a TALE of
HIGHLY
UNUSUAL
MAGIC

a TALE of HIGHLY UNUSUAL MAGIC

by Lisa Papademetriou

SCHOLASTIC INC.

ISBN 978-1-338-03070-9

12 11 10 9 8 7 6 5 4 3 2 1   16 17 18 19 20 21

Printed in the U.S.A.   40

First Scholastic printing, January 2016

Typography by Sarah Creech

This book is dedicated to my daughter,

Zara Marguerite Usman,

with love and extra magic.

a TALE of
HIGHLY
UNUSUAL
MAGIC

Author's Note

I HAVE A MAGIC BOOK.

Let me tell you how it found me. My great-grandfather was German. During the First World War, he was stationed in France. He missed his family a great deal, and one day, he bought a gift for his then six-year-old daughter, my omi (grandmother). It was a book of fairy tales, written in English, because that was a language he wanted to encourage.

Omi was the only member of her family to emigrate. She and her Greek husband moved first to England and later to the United States, escaping Germany just before the outbreak of the Second World War. She brought the book with her, where it sat on a shelf in New Jersey, waiting.

When I was ten years old, my parents separated. That summer, probably to help me escape the misery that hung through our house like fog, my parents sent me to visit Omi. As a birthday present, my grandmother gave the book to me.

Being a girl with a vivid imagination, I knew immediately that the book was magic. The royal blue covers decorated with golden fairies held an elegant, old-fashioned volume of fairy tales, many of which were unknown to me. The full-color illustrations were beautiful, each set on its own special sheet of creamy smooth paper. The stories were written in elegant Victorian style, and when I ran my fingers across the type, I could feel the letter-shaped craters left by the old metal press. Those words gave me an enormous sense of comfort from the universe; their antiquity was a reminder that the book had come to me across continents and decades and landed at the very moment I needed a little magic.

When I was in high school, my friend said to me, "Lisa, isn't it comforting to think that, right now, God is preparing someone special, just for you?" We had been talking about finding the perfect husband. I replied, "But what if that one special person for me is in Japan? What if I never meet him?" My friend rolled her eyes, but the joke is on her: at that very moment, my future husband was in Lahore, Pakistan. The joke was on me, too: I *did* meet him. That's the way magic is. My husband, Ali, was meant for me the same way my book was meant for me. We belonged together: it was fate.

I have heard of a Chinese legend that the gods use a red thread to connect lovers who are destined for each other. I imagine all of us as points that exist in space and time, with red threads that unite us to our important people, places, events, and even things. These threads cross and intersect. They tangle. They are a huge web that circles the world.

Stories are the way we reveal these threads. *This happened, and because of that, this.* This is the way human beings understand ourselves and how we have come to be who we are; narratives show us what is important in our lives. Stories make the magic of fate visible.

My magic book is the way my great-grandfather managed to reach me—his American granddaughter, someone he never knew—across time. He bought the book for Omi, but it was meant for me.

Note

THIS IS A WORK of fiction. Any similarity to persons, living or dead, or actual events is entirely coincidental.

Except for the magic parts.

Those are real.

CHAPTER ONE

Kai

NOBODY HAD EVER TOLD Kai that she should hold her breath when passing by a graveyard, but she did it anyway. She held it and gripped the door handle of the massive powder blue 1987 Dodge pickup as her great-aunt barreled bat-crazy past a large iron gate and up the driveway. Kai gaped through the smudgy truck window at ancient crosses and crumbling white grave markers that hunched, lurking, behind the sagging iron gate. "You live by a graveyard?" she asked, squeezing the door handle like she might just jump out.

"Quiet neighbors!" Great-Aunt Lavinia yelled so Kai could hear her over the Jay-Z song blaring through the radio. The Big Ol' Truck spat gravel as Lavinia slammed the brakes, lurching to a stop. She leaned against the steering wheel and turned to face Kai. "And they never complain about my music." Lavinia cranked up the volume for a moment, rapping along, then switched it off with a wink. "Most people round here like country, but I can't stand it."

"Okay," Kai said, because she thought she should say something. Conversation wasn't really her strongest subject, to tell you the truth.

"You like country?"

"Uh, no."

"Well, all right, because you ain't gonna hear much of it in my house." Lavinia yanked open the door and spilled out. With a deft move, she put one foot on top of the rear tire and hauled herself over the edge of the cargo bed, grabbing Kai's bag and violin case.

Kai wasn't nearly as swift—or as smooth. Gingerly, she pulled back the handle and looked down at the gravel driveway. It seemed like it was about forty feet below her.

"Do you need me to come and get you, sugar?" Lavinia called from the front steps.

"Coming." Clinging to the door, Kai managed to awkwardly half swing, half sprawl onto the pavement. She dusted off her hands and slammed the truck door, giving it a pat as she hurried toward the house.

And what a house!

It had a high peaked roof, and a front porch that had been nearly swallowed up by creeping vines and aggressive shrubbery. A bush with flowers big enough to sit in bloomed just beyond the vines' reach. Everything seemed to join together at odd, tilted angles, as if the house had come home late and rumpled from a particularly wild House Party. A tired picket fence lined the property, and a crooked gate complained at every breeze. The whole place looked like it belonged in a book, but perhaps one that wasn't very nice. I'm talking one where the children get gobbled up in the end.

A mailbox crouched at the end of the footpath. A name was painted on the sign in elegant silver letters. *Quirk,* it read.

You got that right, Kai thought.

So far, her great-aunt Lavinia was a bit . . . odd.

"Your father always called her Auntie Lavinia, but she's actually your great-great-grandfather's cousin, so she must be eighty or ninety years old by now," Kai's mother,

Schuyler, had said right before putting Kai on a plane. "She probably needs a lot of help around the house, the poor, frail old thing. You'll try to be helpful, won't you?"

Let me tell you that Great-Aunt Lavinia was about as frail as a Sherman tank. Kai was never good at judging heights, but I am, and I can tell you that Lavinia was over six feet tall. She carried Kai's suitcase like it was a pocketbook. Kai guessed that she was sixty, but this was one thing that Kai's mother had right: Lavinia would turn eighty-seven at the end of the summer. She had a few wrinkles at the corners of her mouth and eyes, and she had gray hair. But the gray hair was long, almost down to her waist, and held back in a thick braid. Lavinia wore jeans. Not the grandma kind, either, but dark-wash skinny jeans, and red Converse sneakers. Her fingers were full of chunky turquoise jewelry. She looked hip and fashionable, despite the fact that she was shaped a bit like a turnip and one of her eyes was bigger than the other.

This lady, Kai thought as she trotted after her great-aunt, *does* not *need my help around the house.*

Kai hesitated in the doorway a moment, but Lavinia was already jogging up the wide wooden staircase, calling,

"Your room is up here, sweets!"

Kai followed, but she didn't hurry. She ran her hand along the dark banister. It was the kind she had always wished for—perfect for sliding down. Back home, Kai lived in a square gray apartment building with an unreliable elevator.

At the top of the landing, Kai found a long hallway. "This one here is the guest room." Lavinia's voice floated to her from a room on the right. Kai followed the sound and stepped into a lovely white room with a dark wood four-poster bed and matching bureau. An old, smoky mirror reflected gentle light, and crammed bookshelves lined an entire wall. An overstuffed chair lounged in the corner near a window seat that overlooked the front lawn. At home, Kai slept on a mattress on the floor, and shoved her clothes into oversize plastic storage boxes. Her mother didn't believe in spending money on furniture— every spare penny went to Kai's college fund. To Kai, this seemed like a room from a magazine, or a pleasant dream.

"Two other bedrooms up here. Mine's across the hall. One next to it's my office." Lavinia looked around, searching for a good place to put the luggage. "This here room's probably thrilled to have a guest."

"Pretty," Kai said.

"Ain't it?" Lavinia put the suitcase down by the bed and turned to face Kai. "So, listen. I don't know how to say this, so I'm just gonna come out and say it. I can't help it if it hurts your feelings." Lavinia's fingertips dipped into the smallest pocket of her jeans. "I never did have kids. No husband, either. That's 'cause I never wanted to, not 'cause I didn't have offers." Her larger eye bulged out knowingly and her eyebrows danced.

"Okay."

"I don't know what to do with kids."

"Me, either."

Lavinia cocked her head, as if she couldn't tell whether or not Kai was teasing her. She wasn't. Kai really didn't get most kids. They didn't get her, either.

Unlike her peers, she didn't care much about gossip or crushes or screaming worship of the latest boy singer or movie star. She didn't even have *time* for friends, anyway. Not really.

That was something none of her schoolmates under-stood: that Kai had something else that was more

6

important than friends. She had a goal. *Or at least,* she thought, *I used to.*

In fact, the last week of school before summer vacation, someone had posted flyers all over the sixth-grade hall: *The Cedar Creek Stealthy Awards!* Anika Walters won Hottest Girl (of course), Mr. Anderson won Hottest Teacher (surprising), Claire McGowen won Most Likely to Rob a 7-Eleven (duh—she probably already had), and Kai Grove won Weirdest (sigh). When she saw the list, the principal flipped out, and said the class trip to the amusement park would be canceled unless someone came forward to confess or rat out the person who made up the awards. And so Kai was publicly insulted *and* punished along with everyone else, which, according to the principal, "Should teach you all a valuable lesson about life."

"All right, sugar." Lavinia gave Kai a pat on the arm. "I'm just going to do . . . what I do. I'm not going to entertain you."

"Fine. Great, actually."

Lavinia stood perfectly still for a moment. So did Kai. Around them, the house was enormous and silent. "Okay, then," Lavinia said at last. "There's food in the fridge. I don't keep any soda or junk, though. If you want that stuff, you can go walk to the Walgreens."

"By myself?"

"Why not? You're twelve, ain't ya? I was walkin' to the store by myself at age five."

The thought of walking around in a strange town all alone made Kai feel fizzy, like a can of soda that's been shaken up. "Where's the Walgreens?"

"Five blocks." Lavinia yanked her thumb over her shoulder, toward the window behind her, which overlooked the yard. "You can go wherever you want, as long as you're home for dinner. I don't want to have to call your mom and tell her that I lost you."

Excellent point, Kai thought as the fizzy feeling swooshed down to her toes and out to the ends of her hair. "What time is dinner?"

"Six."

"Can I poke around the house?"

"Suit yourself." Lavinia fussed with a curtain for a moment, and then she walked out of the room.

Kai turned to her bags. "Stop looking at me," she muttered as she nudged her violin case with her foot, pushing it into the closet and shutting the door. Sighing, she hauled her suitcase onto a low table but left it closed. She stood beside the window for a moment, just smelling the air in the room. It smelled like clean, old things. White linens lay crisp across the bed. She walked over and scanned the books on the shelves. They didn't seem to be arranged in any order. Paperbacks and hardcovers comingled, with a title about art seated beside a cheap crime novel. A leather-bound book with gold lettering on the spine caught her eye. *The Exquisite Corpse,* it said. Kai pulled it out. She didn't mind creepy titles. She kind of liked them, in fact.

The title was stamped in gold on the front cover, in that curlicue-style writing that people these days think of as "old-fashioned." Below the title was the image of a skeleton hand holding a plumed pen. Instead of an author, it listed Exquisite Corpse Co., Kalamazoo, MI. She flipped through the book, but the thick, gold-beveled pages were blank. *Hm,* she thought, *peculiar.*

Flipping through more slowly, she realized that there was a proper title page (again, no author) and one page of print.

Greetings, salutations, and welcome to the Exquisite Corpse! Just as your grandmother and grandfather used to play the old parlor game in which one person would draw a head, and then fold it over, and another would draw a body, and another would draw legs, and so on—you will breathe life into a creature of your own making. You are about to embark on a journey of magic beyond your powers of discernment, imagination, and belief! All it takes is one person bold enough to set the story in motion!

Let the magic begin!

Beneath this, someone with excellent handwriting had written the name Ralph T. Flabbergast.

There was something about the book that made her shaken-up feeling come back again. And then Kai did something that she never really understood. She pulled a pen from her pocket. After *Ralph T. Flabbergast*, she wrote, *was a complete fool.*

She looked down at the page, dread pricking across her skin on little insect feet. *I shouldn't have done that,* she thought. *That was rude.* Not that Ralph was likely to care. He'd been dead for almost fifty years.

Kai shut the book and put it back onto the shelf. She stared at the gold letters on the spine for a moment, and then turned away.

Outside, the sun shone bright and high. She had been sitting in an airplane for almost four hours, which made her restless. There was no reason to stay indoors. Kai decided to go explore the neighborhood.

It was her second mistake.

CHAPTER TWO

Leila

IT WAS NOT GRAND, but Leila thought it was the most elegant room in the world. She had never been in a private library before. The closest thing at her house was the basement, where there was a sagging bookshelf, a TV, and a decrepit Ping-Pong table. Her mother preferred reading on a Kindle. Her dad only read articles online. They were not romantic people. Leila doubted they would have appreciated a classy room like this one. She wondered if everyone in Pakistan had a library in the house.

Yes, you heard me: Pakistan.

I know, I know—you're thinking, *What? We were just in the United States! Has this narrator lost her mind? Why is she going off on a whole new story?*

Well, that's my own business. Maybe you'll figure it out.

Maybe you won't.

That all depends on you, now, doesn't it?

The walls were curved, as if the library were in a tower, and there was a lovely window seat that looked out onto the garden. Leather- and cloth-bound hardcover books, as still and straight as soldiers, lined the dark wood shelves. A massive wooden desk, richly carved with lions and men in turbans astride horses, stood to one side of the bay window. *I could write a novel at that desk,* Leila thought. *A really thick novel!*

The whole thing was old-fashioned and charming and absolutely not what she had expected to find. She felt like a princess, or like one of the characters in her favorite book series, Dear Sisters. In fact, she felt *exactly* like Elizabeth Dear, the bookish (yet still beautiful) sister, in the story where the two girls went to England and Elizabeth fell in love with someone who she *thought* was a stable boy, but who was really the son of an earl.

"Oh, I do *so* adore a library," Leila said aloud in a truly awful English accent, thinking about how much she would love to have an adventure like Elizabeth's. And in Pakistan, maybe she would! At least here, she had a chance. Back home in the suburbs, it was impossible.

Leila perused the shelves, hoping to discover a few *good* books. Most of these looked dead boring, like the ones her "academically gifted" younger sister, Nadia, liked to read. *Depth of a River. Tom Wickersham. The Pealburl Papers.*

So remarkable, her sister, everyone gushed. *So talented! Nadia Awan is the most brilliant girl at school!*

Ugh, Leila thought. *Nadia Awan is so dull.*

She scanned to the end of a shelf, where her eye fell on one with a catchy title, *The Exquisite Corpse.*

A corpse sounds promising, she thought. She liked mysteries, especially if they involved a girl detective. She reached for the spine, and then hesitated. After all, this wasn't her house. It was her uncle's house, but he probably wouldn't mind. *Then again, what if he does? Maybe I should ask. . . .*

"Yes or no, girl? Don't stand about like an indecisive sheep!"

Leila screeched, whipping around. "W-w-what?" she stammered, staring at the man who had suddenly appeared behind her.

The man pursed his lips, pointing his silver mustache

at the bookshelf. He wore a brown three-piece suit and brown bowler hat, and was definitely not her uncle. Her jaw dangled as she struggled to make sense of this man's presence, his outfit, and his accent, all at once. To her jet-lagged brain, the man's accent had sounded like, "Don stun aboo lie an indessclive ship!"

"I'm sorry, I don't speak Urdu," Leila told him.

"For heaven's sake!" The old man huffed, straightening his blue tie. "Don't you understand English when you hear it? Idiot!"

"What?" Leila asked again. She had understood the words "English" and "idiot," but that was it.

The man leaned on his cane and flashed his dark eyes at her. "Don't just stand there like a fool," he said, deliberately and slowly. "If you want the book, then you should take it!"

Well, once he slowed down, the words finally managed to reach something deep in Leila's brain. "Oh!" she said. "You *are* speaking English."

The man looked as if he had a very low opinion of her. "If you want a book," he said again, "take one."

"I don't really want a book."

He scoffed. "Of course you do." He rapped on the floor with a silver-handled cane. Leila looked back at the book. She looked at the old man. She had no idea who he was, but she was fairly certain of one thing—he did not live in this house. Yesterday, the entire family had come to pick her up at the Lahore airport: her uncle, Babar Awan; his wife; and their three children. And now, here was some old man in a three-piece suit in the family library. *Should I call 911?* she wondered. Could she even use 911 in Pakistan? (Just to let you know: the number is 1122. But if you can't remember that, and you're having an emergency in Pakistan, just yell real loud.)

It finally occurred to her to yell real loud, but Samir—her cousin who was only five months older than she was—walked right in and said, "Oh, hi, Leila. I see you've met Mamoo."

Mamoo is the Urdu word for "uncle." Actually, it's the Urdu word for "my mother's brother." There's a different word for "my father's older brother" (*taya*) and "my father's younger brother" (*chacha*). With a mother, there's just mamoo.

This mamoo looked disgusted. "She's too shy to take a book!"

Leila squirmed.

"What sort of book would you like?" Samir asked.

"I don't really—"

"Where's your father?" Mamoo narrowed his eyes at Samir. "The man spends all of his time ignoring me."

"He's at work, Mamoo," Samir replied. "It's Wednesday. He'll be home at dinnertime."

"Oh, he will, will he?" Mamoo stroked his mustache. Leila thought that he sounded like he didn't believe it, which—I can tell you—he did *not*. "I'll be back at nine o'clock sharp. But don't tell him I'm coming!" He scowled at Leila.

"*I'm* not gonna tell him," she said.

"He really isn't avoiding you, Mamoo," Samir called down the hallway.

The old man shook his cane, but didn't turn back.

Samir faced Leila. He pushed his rectangular glasses farther up his long nose. One of his thick black eyebrows was permanently arched, which made it look as if he was mocking the world. People often took that eyebrow personally. Right now, Samir was looking at Leila's hair, which made her smooth it self-consciously. "What sort of book were you looking for?"

"I . . . I just . . ." Leila blushed a little under Samir's gaze. If only she were Elizabeth Dear! Then she would have thought of something witty and charming, yet utterly unassuming, to say. Even Nadia could have spouted some kind of Noteworthy Quotation from a Literary Luminary about the Importance of Story.

But Leila was stuck being herself, and all she came up with was, "I like all different kinds of books. I wasn't looking for anything in particular."

"Take any book you want," Samir told her.

Leila's father was from Pakistan, and she knew one thing for sure about the culture—if someone thought you wanted something, be it a pancake or a bar of gold—they would insist that you take it from them. They would insist *forever*. Pakistani hospitality is an irresistible force and an immovable object rolled into one. There was really only one way to solve the problem. She grabbed *The Exquisite Corpse* from the shelf and mumbled thanks.

They stood in silence for a moment, as perfectly still

as the shelves around them. "Do you like reading?" Samir asked at last.

"Of course. I read all the time."

"Kim's gun is on display here in Lahore, if you'd like to see it." Leila's face was blank, so he added, "*Kim*, by Rudyard Kipling. Kipling used to live in Lahore. Have you read it?"

"No."

"Oh. *The Jungle Book*? The *Just So Stories*?"

"I know *The Jungle Book*," she said. She didn't want to admit that she had never heard of Kipling. She'd always thought that Walt Disney wrote the movie.

"They make us read Kipling in my school, since he lived here and won the Nobel Prize. What was the last book you read?"

"*Sweeter than Sugar*," Leila said. It was #32 in the Dear Sisters series. "It's really good," she added, wondering if she sounded as intelligent as Elizabeth Dear.

"I'm sure it is," Samir said with that arched eyebrow. "We could go see the gun, if you like."

Now, Leila had about as much desire to go see a gun previously owned by Kipling as she had to mop up a hairball made by her cat, Steve. But Samir's brown eyes were gleaming, and Leila sensed that this was some famous Pakistani thing she was supposed to be all excited about, so she said, "Okay. Sounds great." Leila hated to hurt people's feelings.

"Oh, by the way," Samir added as she started to turn away. "Rabeea was looking for you earlier. I think that she and my mom want to take you shopping. They said that you wanted some *salwar kameez*."

"Yes!" Leila cried. "I love Pakistani clothes, but I never get a chance to wear them at home. Where's Rabeea?"

Samir directed her to the front sitting room, and she hurried away. Leila rounded the corner so quickly that she nearly ran into someone. "Oh, sorry!" Leila gasped.

This was Chirragh Baba, the cook. He said something sharp in Punjabi. He had the sort of face you would draw with heavy lines—wrinkles ran from his large, long nose to his puckered mouth, as if he had done a lot of frowning in his life. (He had.) His hair was dark orange—henna dye over gray—and his black eyes seemed to lead down a deep, deep well. They were eyes to nowhere. Leila had met Chirragh the night before, and he had given Leila an unwelcoming welcome.

"How long is she staying?" Chirragh had demanded,

scowling. He'd said it in Punjabi, of course, but seven-year-old Wali had helpfully translated for Leila.

Now, Chirragh's eyes glittered like something that just might bite you. It was his signature look. He reminded Leila of the evil butler in *Dear Sisters Super Special #8: The Case of the Creepy Castle*. That guy had been super-duper bad news.

"Uh, sorry," Leila muttered again. She looked down at her shoes, avoiding that disturbing dark gaze.

Chirragh didn't speak another word, but continued limping down the stairs, supporting himself on his strong, right leg.

Leila looked up and watched him go. *I'd better keep an eye on him,* she thought, half hoping that he would turn out to be a major villain—maybe stealing spoons or spreading false rumors. That would open up a lot of adventure possiblities!

She stopped by her room and put the book at the edge of her bed. *The Exquisite Corpse. Definitely a mystery,* she decided. Leila knew that Elizabeth Dear wouldn't be in it. Still, she was hopeful that it would be both utterly romantic and moderately gruesome.

She couldn't wait to read it.

CHAPTER THREE

Kai

KAI SHOULD NOT HAVE gone to the Walgreens. Like I said, that was her second mistake. Oh, she still would have had an adventure—writing in the book guaranteed it. But it might have been a smaller adventure. Oh, well. She went, so it wasn't.

It was five *long* blocks to the Walgreens pharmacy. In the gutter, Kai saw a squashed frog that had dried to leather in the Texas heat. I like to call that road jerky. A thick breeze licked at her sweaty scalp. The lawns were patched with grass so dry and brown it looked like hay.

Across the sidewalk, Kai's flip-flops *shlip-shlip-shliped* after her. She was the only pedestrian in sight. Everyone else was locked up tight in their cars breathing nothing but air-conditioning, like people who were used to serious heat and didn't want to put up a pointless fight.

She paused at the stoplight, and looked up the street, to where the black ribbon of asphalt bled against the wavy edge of the sky. It was so hot that the tar patching the cracks in the road had melted, and lay there soft as warm candle wax. When the white letters lit up, she scurried across the intersection, wisely wary. That tar would've grabbed her flip-flop and ripped it right off her foot. Then she'd have had to run out into traffic to try to get it back. Probably would've gotten run over by a Chevy Suburban, which would have made this into a very different kind of story. Much shorter.

Kai scuttled across the parking lot and onto the wide sidewalk that bordered the strip mall. There it was: the Walgreens. The air-conditioned home of Dr Pepper and Cheetos. Heaven for the kind of girl who was never let out of the house by herself, which—let me tell you—is the kind of girl she was. She even considered buying *two* bags of Cheetos. That's how big this adventure was to Kai.

Two newspaper boxes stood sentry outside the double glass doors. A dog leash looped, loose and limp, around one. At the bottom, panting in the shadow of the strip mall's roof, lay an exhausted-looking brown-and-white

Chihuahua. His tiny tongue lolled from the side of his mouth, and his tan ribs rose and fell in quick time.

"Hey, cutie," Kai said, stooping to doggie level.

"You shouldn't pet strange dogs."

Kai looked up. A girl with curly black hair and eight million freckles poked her head around the side of a stucco pillar. "Didn't your mother ever teach you that?" the girl asked.

This chafed at Kai like a burlap backpack. First of all, her mother *had* told her that. But her mother never let her do *anything*. Second, this girl looked like one of the Bunnies—the pretty girls—at her school, who always thought they knew everything, but who really had brains like vacant parking lots. And third, this dog was *tiny*. He weighed about an ounce; how much damage could he do? Kai ignored the freckled girl and touched the tip of the dog's ear with a single finger.

That Chihuahua burst like a firecracker! He snarled and snapped at Kai, who screamed and fell backward onto her butt. The dog barked like it was fighting off a shark attack, and a woman in a muumuu blasted out of the electronic door shouting, "Taco! Taco!"

But Taco had already lurched to the end of his leash and clamped his jaws onto the hem of Kai's jeans.

"Get him off!" Kai screamed.

"Taco!" the woman shouted. Her giant blonde hair quivered with each screech. "Taco!"

The freckle-faced girl walked over and grabbed the dog by the scruff of the neck. She gave him a good shake until he let go. Then she handed him to the woman with the giant hair, who said, "Oh, Taco, you naughty baby," and nuzzled him adoringly. She turned to Kai and shouted, "What're you pestering my dog for?"

"Why did you leave your dangerous dog unattended?" the freckled girl demanded. "Taco needs a muzzle. My dad's a lawyer—you'll be lucky if we don't sue. I'll bet Taco's done this before—hasn't he?"

The woman with the giant hair huffed and walked off, cooing to Taco as he licked her on the neck.

Kai stood up and silently watched the woman stuff herself into a small Honda. The dog rode shotgun. Then she turned to face the girl with the freckles.

"I'm Doodle," the girl said. "And you're welcome."

Kai—who had just been about to say thank you—was

irritated again. Bunnies always had cutesy nicknames, and this one was no exception. "Why Doodle? Are you an artist, or something?" she demanded.

"I was born on the Fourth of July."

Kai frowned. "Does that explain something?"

Doodle started humming "Yankee Doodle Dandy." Kai had never heard anyone hum in a way that made it sound like, "*Duh-uh-uh-uh-uh-uh-DUH-DUH . . .*"

"Oh," Kai said, feeling even more irritated and stupid than before. "Well, yeah—thanks for saving me from that Chihuahua."

Doodle smirked a little. She had a twitchy little mouth, and her smirks were rather comical. Everyone thought so, not just me.

"What's so funny?"

"Do you think they have a card for that? In the drugstore—'Thank you for saving me from that Chihuahua.' With, like, a rose on it? Everything written out in gold letters, all scripty, and a poem inside?"

"Yeah, they probably sell a lot of them," Kai said. "At this location, anyway. Well, see you around." She turned toward the doors. The electronic eye sensed her movement and opened for her, blasting her with cold air.

"Hey—" Doodle called after her, "what's your name?"

For a second, Kai was tempted to pretend that she hadn't heard. Her mother always said she should never tell strangers her name. Then again, she thought that she'd probably never see this girl again, so who cared? "Kai!" she called, a moment before the doors closed behind her.

Doodle's funny, twitchy mouth smiled at her through the glass.

Kai didn't know what to think of that smile. Yet. But I was confident she would figure it out.

It was the same long walk back in the opposite direction, only—this time—Kai didn't have air-conditioning to look forward to. She'd hung around the magazine racks until the skinny, acne-faced clerk came over and started arranging them protectively. Then Kai wandered around the aisles for a while until the same clerk started following her, eyeing her pockets suspiciously. Finally, she had to admit that it was time to go back outside.

Kai felt the air-conditioning evaporate right off her clothes the minute the electronic door opened. The air shimmered with the sound of cicadas as she started for Lavinia's house. The good news was that the queasy feeling left over from the airplane had disappeared. Walking had helped.

She heard the argument before she saw it, but wouldn't you know, the minute she was within spitting distance of Lavinia's house, Kai saw a certain curly-haired, freckle-faced girl facing a smirking boy with eyes like steel. The boy was taller than Doodle, and if Kai were the type to admit it, handsome. His clothes were fashionably large and new looking, and everything about him seemed to say "I'M RICH" in all capital letters, just like that. The boy was holding something. A jar.

"Give it back, Pettyfer," Doodle demanded. But she said it in a way that didn't sound too hopeful. "You'll damage it."

"Damage it?" Pettyfer laughed, shaking the jar. "It's already damaged. What do you want it for, anyway?" He shook it again. Kai could see that there was a bug inside.

Doodle reached for the jar, and Pettyfer yanked it away. And Kai—who never really spoke up to anyone—stepped forward and shouted, "Hey!"

Pettyfer stopped and stared at her.

Now, Kai wasn't a big girl. She wasn't particularly good at fighting. But she was good at *planning*. The kids at school thought she was weird, but they didn't really pick on her because she had hundreds of prewritten comeback lines and always mapped out her route between classes to avoid the biggest bullies. Kai came from a big city, and she had a plan for almost everything. Her plan for people who wanted to rob her or threaten her was this: *Make them think you're dangerously crazed.* So when Pettyfer looked at her, she grabbed two fistfuls of her own hair and *roared*, then charged directly at him, screaming, "Yi-yi-yi-yi-yi-yi-yiiiiiiiiiiiii!"

Pettyfer fell over backward, scrambled to his feet, and took off, tripping over his enormous, expensive shoes.

"Yi-yi-yi-yi-yi-EEEEEEEEEEEEEEEEEEEEEE-OOOOOOOOO! Blooga-blooga! Blooga-blooga!"

"Aaaaaaah!" Pettyfer screamed and picked up speed. He had to hold up his baggy jeans as he ran. In about a half a second, he had disappeared behind a neighboring house.

Panting, Kai came to a stop beside Doodle, who was staring at her, bug-eyed. Kai put her hands on her knees, bending over to suck in a deep breath. "Whoa," Doodle said.

Kai looked up at her. "He wasn't expecting that," she explained.

"*Nobody* was expecting that," Doodle replied. "Ever."

"Is your butterfly okay?" Kai asked as Doodle bent over to retrieve the jar. It was made of plastic, and had only bounced when Pettyfer dropped it.

Doodle held up the jar. "It's a moth," she said. "And it was dead when I found it." She shook her head. "I'd wanted to see if I could identify it, but it's too messed up now." She unscrewed the top and shook out the moth, which dropped to the ground just like an old piece of lint, not like something that used to live, and breathe, and fly.

"Who was that guy and why was he trying to steal your dead moth?" Kai asked. "And why were you carrying around a dead moth in the first place?"

"I'm a lepidopterist," Doodle said.

Kai thought this over. "Is that contagious?"

Doodle didn't exactly laugh, but her eyes squinched up as if maybe she was thinking about it. "That's someone who studies butterflies and moths. I'm into moths, mostly."

"Is that . . . interesting?"

"It is to me."

"Oh." Kai squinted at the limp form on the grass—the dead moth. She could see how moths might be interesting. To the right person. "Why was that boy trying to take it from you?"

"Because he likes to destroy stuff he doesn't understand, which is just about everything."

Kai nodded. She knew the type. (Don't we all?)

"Everyone in school is afraid of him because his family's rich." Doodle screwed the lid back onto the jar, and she and Kai fell into step toward the sidewalk. "They own the casket factory."

"Glamorous."

Doodle shrugged. "They employ half the town, it seems like. And they always have clients, so . . ."

"Right."

The girls looked at each other. Kai was beginning to think that maybe Doodle wasn't a Bunny, after all. Bunnies are pretty on the outside, hollow on the inside, like a chocolate Easter Rabbit. But Doodle was starting to seem . . . solid.

"So—who are you? Where do you live?" Doodle asked.

"That one." Kai pointed to the strange, stooped house that was perched way back on the lawn, as if considering its own property.

"The Quirk House?"

Kai knew that Quirk was her aunt's last name. Still, it sounded kind of funny, now that she heard it out loud. It sounded as if the whole *house* was quirky, which it was. "She's my great-aunt. Well, my great-great-grandfather's cousin, actually. But I'm going with great-aunt."

"Wow—I didn't realize Lavinia had any family. Alive, I mean." Doodle's voice held a strange mix of surprise and relief. "I live right there, across the street." She pointed to a small ranch house with the driest, deadest grass that Kai had ever seen. There was a single scrawny bush in the front that was so thorny it looked like it could only dream of roses.

"Guess I'll be seeing a lot of you, then," Kai said.

"Maybe so." Doodle looked down at her jar. "Hey— what are you doing after dinner?"

"Nothing. Why?" Kai was hoping Doodle might want

to go to the movies. Kai loved movies. She and her mom went every week.

Doodle grinned. "Want to help me catch a moth?"

When she thought about it afterward, Kai was never really sure why she said yes. Maybe it was because she and Doodle had bonded—they had each saved the other from something vicious and ridiculous. Or maybe because it was hard to pass up the idea of going hunting for something that had been extinct since 1882.

Yes, that's right. Doodle didn't just want to find any old moth. She wanted to find a *particular* moth. A moth that didn't exist: the Celestial Moth. The last recorded sighting in Falls River, Texas, was by a woman named Edwina Pickle.

"Extirpation," Doodle had explained.

Kai frowned. "You know a lot of . . . words."

Kai knew a lot of words, too, but *extirpation* was new.

"That means it's extinct, but just around here. You can still find them in other parts of the world."

"So what makes you think we'll find one here? Now?" Kai had asked.

Doodle shrugged. "Just a feeling. Stuff is going un-extinct all the time."

"Like what?"

"Like Miller's Grizzled Langurs."

"That sounds like something on a fancy dinner menu. *I'd like the grizzled langur in chipotle sauce, please.*"

"It's a primate. A monkey in Indonesia. Scientists thought it was extinct, and then they found some. So maybe the problem with this moth isn't that it's extinct. Maybe the problem is that nobody's been looking for it." Doodle grinned. "Nobody except me. So nobody's gonna find it . . . except me. I've got a good feeling about it."

Kai had to admit that there were probably not a lot of people out looking for this particular moth. Personally, she had never gone looking for *any* moths, or heard of anyone who did. So she said okay. She said that she would see Doodle later, as long as Lavinia said it was okay to go on a moth hunt.

Kai clomped up the stairs to lie down for a while before dinner, still giddy from her (very small) adventure.

Kai had never had this kind of freedom before. Her mother always acted as if the city were crawling with drug addicts and child killers, and she wouldn't even let Kai walk to the bodega on the corner by herself.

Kai reached for her suitcase (she still hadn't unpacked) and plopped it onto her bed. As she unzipped the top, she noticed something peeking out from beneath her pillow. It was the corner of a book. She shoved the pillow aside. Old-fashioned gold letters spelled out *The Exquisite Corpse*.

Weird! She didn't remember putting it there.

She flipped it open and nearly dropped it again.

Someone had written in it. Right after *Ralph T. Flabbergast was a complete fool*, someone had added,

Yes, Ralph was a fool. But he didn't know it.

You see, Ralph believed in magic. He believed in it with his whole heart. He had ever since he was a small boy, when his oma told the most magical stories of fairies and talking beasts. He loved his grandmother dearly, and cried bitterly when she died, although he was only three years old and everyone said he was too young to understand what death meant. Four years later, he still remembered the smell of her kitchen and the feeling he had whenever she told her tales.

One sultry afternoon, he shuffled down a hot city side-walk with a nickel in his pocket. Ralph had a problem: only one nickel, and so many ways to spend it. The smell of hot pretzels wafted over to him. Jewel-colored candies smiled at him from behind a glass window. Toys and whistles, chestnuts, or a movie. It was a torment.

"Roll up, roll up, roll up, and see if you can find the ball beneath the magic shell! Winner doubles his money! How about you, young lad?" The man had a long nose and large teeth, and looked rather like a horse in a top hat. It was impossible to be suspicious of a man who looked like that.

"What's this?" Ralph asked, so the man explained the game. There were three walnut shells and a pea. The man placed the pea under one of the shells, and then mixed them up.

"You tell me where the pea is," the man said, "and you're a winner! Double your money!"

Ralph watched the shells weave in and out, back and forth. It was like a dance. A slow, gentle dance. He pointed to a shell, and the man turned it over. There was the pea. This is easy! Ralph thought as he handed over his nickel for another try.

"Are you ready?" The man made the walnuts dance. Ralph watched. He pointed. There was the pea.

"A winner!" the man crowed. "Really, son, that was amazing. Most people can't keep their eyes on the shell at all. You're a natural, you are."

Ralph held out his palm, but the man said, "Blasted if you don't get another try for your nickel. Well, I'm a fool to let you do it. You'll have another dime off of me, and no mistake. I don't suppose you want to just walk away now?" The man took off his top hat and held it over his heart, revealing a pasty, bald scalp covered with scraggly black threads of hair.

Ralph laughed. He had never been good at anything in his life! "I think I'll play again," he said.

The man placed the pea beneath the center shell and made the walnuts dance. Faster and faster, like a mad jig. But Ralph kept his eyes on the shell. He knew it. He knew it. The man stopped. Ralph pointed. The man lifted the shell. The pea was gone. "Sorry, son," the man said. "Would you like another go?"

"I don't have any more money."

"Ah, rough luck."

Emotion washed over Ralph as he stood, immobile, watching the man put away his shells. I know what you're thinking: sadness, misery, disappointment. But you're wrong. You see, Ralph had seen something. Something that changed his life. When the man lifted the shells, the pea wasn't under any of them.

Ralph's world tilted on its axis. The sky tore open above him, revealing a white light.

Never mind the nickel. Never mind.

He had seen magic.

Kai flipped through more pages. They were blank.

She slammed the book shut. *What the heck was that?*

What the heck?

What the . . .

Lavinia wrote it, she thought. *She must have! But why? To be funny?*

That seemed unlikely. Lavinia didn't seem like the kind of person for practical jokes. She seemed more like a person for practical footwear. Kai looked around the room, wondering if her mysterious great-aunt was about to jump out at her. Slowly and softly, Kai walked over to the closet. With a deep breath, she yanked it open. But the closet was empty, except for the violin case, which lay like a dusty black shadow at the bottom.

Someone sneaked in here and wrote a weird story while I was out, she thought. *Or else I went crazy, wrote this myself, and then forgot all about it.*

Minds are pretty creative things, aren't they? Kai's worked very hard to try to make sense of the story and how it got there. But it was wrong on all counts.

It's a prank, Kai thought. *A stupid prank.* She shut the book and shoved it onto the closet shelf. She yanked on a sweater, commanding herself to stop thinking about the book. *Don't think about it,* her mind said sternly. *Think about the moth, or Doodle. Think about Lavinia.*

But she couldn't. Her mind was consumed with that book and its story for the rest of the afternoon—right up until it was time for dinner.

CHAPTER FOUR

Leila

BEYOND THE WINDOW, THE city of Lahore was dark. *Really* dark, because the power was out. To conserve energy, the local government had instituted "load shedding": rolling blackouts during the cooler hours of the day. Inside the Awan house, though, the rooms were bright and cheerful, thanks to the generators humming in the backyard.

Leila breathed in the heavy scent of masala, nicked with the sharp undercurrent of *gobi* and warm oily *parathas*, like a scratchy blanket. She knew most, but not all, of the dishes on her plate, and she was determined to try everything—even the green stuff. This was part of having "an authentic cultural experience," which was a phrase that Leila had read that afternoon on her sister's blog.

Nadia was in Kenya, as part of a program for

middle-school girls who were gifted in science. She was studying elephants and helping to build a library for a village of very photogenic Kenyans, many of whom were pictured on Nadia's blog, clustered around her while she played her guitar. It wasn't easy to have a younger sister who was in your same grade, and while the blog made Leila feel closer to Nadia, it also made her want to strangle her a little. Nadia just always had to be the fascinating sister, didn't she? It occurred to Leila that she should start a blog, too. But she would need Nadia to help her set it up. Also, the Awans' wireless connection was really spotty, so it would have to wait until she got home. Still, she could take notes. Leila took a bite of green stuff. Hot . . . hot . . . superhot! She downed a full glass of water, which didn't help.

Title for Blog One: Hot Stuff!

Every few minutes, Chirragh limped into the room to slam a new dish onto the table. He only had two facial expressions, Leila noticed: Glaring, and Glaring Furiously. However, he glared at everyone equally, which comforted Leila slightly. Nobody in the Awan family seemed to care, or even notice. They barely registered

Chirragh's existence, much less his feelings.

"It's hot," Rabeea said, adjusting the diaphanous blue *duputa* draped around her shoulders. She fanned herself with her fingers dramatically, making her sleeves flap.

"The air-conditioning is on," her aunt, Jamila Tai, said. "Leila, dear, try the gobi."

Leila didn't usually like cauliflower, but this was creamy and only slightly spicy, delicious enough to make Leila consider adding recipes to her blog.

"Can't we make it cooler?" Rabeea demanded. "It's always stuffy in here. Aren't you hot, Leila?"

"I'm fine," Leila said as a trickle of sweat rolled down her back.

"Are you comfortable, Leila?" Her uncle put down his knife and fork. "I'm sure it's warmer here than you're used to. I can ask Chirragh to cool things down." He looked around for the cook.

"Really, Babar Taya, I'm fine," Leila assured him.

"*I'm* hot!" Wali said. He was seven. Nobody paid him any attention.

"She just doesn't want to hurt your feelings," Rabeea told her mother.

"Rabeea." Jamila Tai's voice was a warning.

Leila hoped that sweat wasn't staining the armpits of her new hot-pink salwar kameez. This afternoon's shopping trip had been a bit of a bust. First, Rabeea and her mother had taken Leila to a fabric store, insisting that she could have whatever she wanted made. Leila had done tons of research on the Internet and had picked out her favorite styles. But every time she pointed to a fabric and described what she wanted, Rabeea would get this weird, tight little smile and explain, "That's not really in fashion right now." And even though she always added, "But you should get it if that's what you want," Leila hadn't come to the other side of the world to look like a dork. So they left that store and went to a place that had ready-made clothes, which culminated in Rabeea and her mother getting into a very polite fight about whether Leila should wear short sleeves.

"It's not appropriate." Jamila Tai frowned at the brilliant blue dress that Rabeea had pulled out.

"She's American," Rabeea had countered. "She can wear what she wants. Besides, all of the girls are wearing sleeveless," Rabeea said.

Jamila Tai smiled, and spoke through clenched teeth. "That is absolutely not true."

"It is true." Rabeea's voice was sweet, but her eyes were narrowed. "What, do you want her to wear *hijab*, too?"

That went on for a while. Leila just watched. This was the same kind of argument that her sister often had with her mother about cell phones. Leila knew that it would not pay to get involved.

She didn't have the energy to argue, anyway. Here is the thing about Lahore in the summer: it's hot. And that day, it was hot like you don't know hot. Even in the air-conditioned store, it was hot. It was the kind of heat that it's hard to recover from.

Have you ever stood near an oven door when someone opened it to check on something that was baking in there? Have you ever been hit with a wave of hot air like that? In Lahore, that was the *breeze*. You actually had to close the windows to keep the wind out. You had to keep the house dark in the daytime.

It was so hot, when she went outside Leila could feel her brain cooking inside her skull, like a boiled egg. It was so hot that the idea of a long-sleeved shirt seemed nuts. Then again, Leila didn't want to stand out as "The American Weirdo." This is a strange fact: in the United States, people thought of Leila as Pakistani. But here, people thought of her as American. With a white mother and a Pakistani father, Leila used to think that she was both. But Leila was beginning to realize that, in some ways, she was also neither. In other people's minds, at least.

Anyway, Leila really didn't care about the sleeves, so she finally just said, "Long-sleeved is fine with me," and Jamila Tai smiled smugly. From the expression on her face, Rabeea obviously wished she could strangle Leila.

So, here Leila was, in her long-sleeved kameez, with Rabeea still clearly outraged by the situation, but not saying so, at least not directly.

Well, maybe The Sleeveless Debate could be Blog Two, Leila mused.

The doorbell rang, but nobody at the table stood up. They just waited for Chirragh or one of the other servants to answer it. After a moment, a fat woman with an enormous, beaming smile walked in. The silk of her bejeweled kameez (sleeveless, by the way, which showed her dimpled arms) fluttered as she walked. She was beyond glamorous, and Leila liked her right away. But she only thought about her for a short moment, because right behind the glamourpuss was the handsomest boy that Leila had ever seen. The minute he walked in, she knew he was the One. She knew it the way Elizabeth Dear knew it the moment she saw the stableboy in *Dreams of England*. And the way Elizabeth knew it when she shook hands with the editor of her school paper, Roland Whiting, in *Paper Tigers*. Oh! And the way Elizabeth knew it when she met the mysterious new barista—Alex James—in *Latte Love*.

He had thick, dark hair that spiked up, like it was thinking mischievous thoughts and might run off at any moment. His long black eyelashes fringed around inky eyes. They were eyes like a night sky—dark, with stars. Oh boy, he was handsome. And he cooked Leila's brain just as good as the hot Pakistani sun, I can tell you. Her brain went straight from hard-boiled to scrambled.

"As-salaam alaikum!" the fat lady sang out, and then everyone got up and salaamed and the women kissed each other on the cheeks.

"Mrs. Haq, I'd like to introduce you to my niece," Babar Taya said, gesturing to Leila. "This is Leila. Leila, this is Mrs. Haq and her son, Zain."

"Salaam, salaam." *Peace, peace.* Leila could speak this much, at least.

"*Ap kitne den Lahore me henh?*" Mrs. Haq's heavily mascaraed eyelashes batted a friendly wave.

"She doesn't speak Urdu." Jamila Tai wore the same tight smile that Rabeea had worn earlier, when Leila had described out-of-date fashions.

"Oh! Your parents never taught you?" Mrs. Haq's face was all smug innocence. "What a shame. And your father is such a brilliant man, *mashallah*."

Jamila Tai muttered something, but the only word Leila caught was *Amrikan*. It was the word that made Zain step forward.

"You're the American!" Zain said, as if being American were wonderful, thrilling, fantastic!

"Yes, but she's still dressed more conservatively than a fundo," Rabeea put in.

Her mother shot her a look that could have melted lead.

Zain laughed. "Not quite a burka," he said, referring to Leila's outfit. Leila wished Rabeea would let it go. Leila

47

thought her clothes were pretty. Hot pink cotton with lovely little beads at the neckline and hem of the kameez, this was easily one of the nicest outfits she had ever owned. And she had three more upstairs, in different colors! True, the last time she had come to Lahore—on a family trip when she was four—her grandmother had spoiled her, dressing her like a princess in a new outfit every four hours. But her grandmother had died when she was five. This time, Leila had to spoil herself, but she wasn't about to complain. It wasn't like they were making her wear a headscarf. Just the floaty duputa, worn around the shoulders unless it was time for prayers. The men wore prayer hats, too, in the mosque. When Leila was seven, she had asked her father why Allah hates looking down at the top of everyone's head. She wondered if he felt the same way about heads that she felt about looking at people's feet.

"So, are they taking you to see any sights while you're here?" Zain asked.

"I want to go to Shalimar Gardens," Leila said, "And Badshahi Mosque, and I want to go for a camel ride."

"A camel ride?" Rabeea said. "There are no camel rides in Lahore."

"Yes!" Wali insisted. "Lahore Zoo!"

"I just want a picture of me riding a camel," Leila said, and Rabeea gave her that same little disapproving smile.

"Perhaps Leila would enjoy the Lahore Museum," Babar Taya suggested.

"And Kim's gun," Samir added. "Leila likes Kipling."

Leila wondered where that had come from. She hadn't said that, had she?

"Do you?" Zain said to her, as if Kipling were a very amusing thing to like. "You should have them take you to the new shopping mall."

"Oh, yes, they've done a lovely job with it," Mrs. Haq agreed. "Marble everywhere!" She gestured wildly, as if to help them all envision the masses of marble.

"Leila doesn't care about a shopping mall." Samir sounded a little irritated.

"Of course she does," Rabeea snapped. "It's air-conditioned."

Leila wondered why everyone seemed to know what she liked, all of a sudden.

"I want to go!" Wali piped up. "Leila will like it; there's a McDonald's!"

Zain laughed, and so did Rabeea. Then Leila laughed a little, too, so as not to be left out. Samir's arched eyebrow lifted another fraction of an inch.

"Well, perhaps we'll all go," Babar Taya began.

"*Inshallah,*" Mrs. Haq said.

"*Inshallah,*" Jamila Tai agreed.

"I know you're there, I can hear your voice!" An eight-foot-tall giant stormed into the dining room as Chirragh scowled behind him. Leila let out a little shriek, and then realized it wasn't a giant, after all. It was Mamoo, in his bowler hat. "You can't avoid me now!"

"As-salaam alaikum, Uncle," Zain said, and soon everyone was greeting the furious man in the three-piece suit. Babar Taya soothed him and offered him a chair, insisting that he hadn't been avoiding Mamoo in the sort of soft voice one uses when diffusing a three-year-old's tantrum.

"Do you think he uses a time machine when he shops for clothes?" Zain murmured, just loudly enough for Leila to hear. She giggled, naturally. He could have said anything, and she would have giggled. As I said: scrambled.

"Oh, hello, Mrs. Haq," Mamoo said. "My, my. What

lovely jewels." He said this without enthusiasm, and Mrs. Haq's eyes narrowed to little slits.

"Hello, Mr. Bilal. How is your work at the university?" Mrs. Haq's voice was like acid, dripping from her lips as if it might burn a hole in the carpet.

Mamoo removed his hat and jutted his chin proudly. "My research is doing quite well, thank you."

"*Mashallah*," Mrs. Haq replied.

Leila had the feeling that, even though most of it was in English, this conversation required a translator. Things were being said, but she didn't know what they meant.

"Well, Zain and I must be going," Mrs. Haq announced. She bid everyone *Allah hafiz* and walked out into the hallway. Zain, smiling apologetically, said good night and followed her. But before he left and before Leila turned back to the table to sit down, he cast a look over his shoulder. It was a smile for Leila. She caught it, like a butterfly in a net. A moment later, he was gone, but a thought remained: *This is it. My adventure! My romance! My future blog! I can't wait to tell Aimee—*

But Leila caught herself. *No*, she thought. *Not Aimee. I'll tell Ta'Mara.* Leila was still getting used to the idea that Aimee was her ex-friend. It was like her jet lag; sometimes her heart felt like it had been left in a different time zone.

A chair was brought for Mamoo and his hat and cane taken away. Everyone settled back down to dinner, and Leila recommenced picking at her food. She felt someone's eyes on her, and when she looked up, she discovered that Rabeea was watching her. She wasn't smiling. When Leila caught her look, Rabeea looked away.

Chirragh stumped out and put a new pile of hot chapatis on the table.

"Lovely, Chirragh Baba!" Mamoo proclaimed, rubbing his hands together. "The best chapatis in Lahore."

Chirragh didn't acknowledge that he had heard, but Leila caught a little smile on his lips as he turned toward the kitchen. For half a moment, he was Not Glaring. Naturally, Leila made a mental note of this. Was Mamoo evil, too? She hoped so! She could bust him in *Blog Three: Villains Revealed!*

Things are happening, Leila thought as she took a red-hot bite of chicken *jalfrezi*. *Things are happening all around me, and I don't know what they are. Yet.*

But she didn't mind. Every good story has a mystery, doesn't it?

A few hours later, Leila sat in the middle of a red coverlet in the guest bedroom, staring at the off-white wall. She had tried to Skype her mom, but got voice mail. Then she dialed her dad, and got voice mail. She left each of them an I-love-you message.

Leila wondered what they were doing. Working? They both worked like crazy. Her mother was a freelance writer and editor who always took on five more projects than she could handle. She was really good at her job, and she loved it, and she had a hard time saying no.

Her father did something with computers that involved a lot of blank staring at a screen and strong black tea.

They were kind people, and had even considered coming along on the trip to Lahore, until they both realized that they had major projects in critical stages that could not just be abandoned for three weeks. Leila loved her parents, even though she sometimes wished they were a little more—extraordinary. Like the parents in books who always seemed to be absentminded geniuses, or super-spies, or evil, or dead. Because who could have an adventure with parents like hers? They were just so *normal* . . .

But she missed them, anyway.

Leila stared up at the ceiling, which was a different shade of white from the ceiling in her room at home, although she couldn't quite say how. The bedroom was strange. It was too big. It had never occurred to Leila that a big bedroom could be a nuisance, but it was. For one thing, the large room made the twin bed and three-drawer bureau seem miniature. For another, it took her twenty-three steps just to get to the closet. Twenty-three! She had counted. That was a long way to go just to hang up a shirt, but her salwar kameez was too nice to just toss on the floor. With a sigh, she hauled herself off the bed and trekked to the closet. Then she changed into her fuzzy Hello Kitty pajama bottoms and an old Waffle Shack T-shirt. She felt better already.

As she made the long journey back to the bed, she noticed the book she had carelessly tossed there earlier. *The Exquisite Corpse.* She had read through it earlier and decided that she had better return it to the library the next day. With the exception of the first sentence, the pages flowed with beautiful, old-fashioned handwriting. This was no gruesome mystery-romance; it was clearly someone's treasure.

Leila opened the window for a moment to let out some of the stale over-conditioned air. The city smelled of smoke, but she still breathed easier with the window open. She looked out, thinking how lucky she was to have a room on the second floor. The house was large, and was surrounded by a garden that would have been quite lush if the sun weren't so harsh and if the wind didn't deposit dust on every leaf. That very morning, while she stood at that very window, Leila had spotted a green parrot perched on a tree. She had assumed it was an escaped pet, like the parakeets she sometimes saw back home. But Rabeea had explained to her that, no, these were wild, and they were everywhere.

But I'm getting off the track again!

Across the street, the dark dome of a mosque blotted out a section of sky. She felt the largeness of the room behind her, the empty space. And, just as she was about to pull the curtains, something fluttered up and over the windowsill and floated toward her bedside lamp. The moth was lovely, silver green and blue, and it perched for a moment on the lip of the shade, perfectly still. But the light was too intoxicating; the moth fluttered again, circling and circling the light, dipping toward the bulb.

"I know it's pretty, but that's not going to end well for you," Leila told the moth. She walked over to the lamp and shut it off. It took a moment for her eyes to adjust to the dim room, but when they did, Leila saw that the moth was luminous—phosphorescent in the fading light. It fluttered around the room for a while, and then turned toward the open window, where it slipped out, seeking light elsewhere.

"You're going to burn yourself up!" Leila called after the moth, but it didn't come back. The moth didn't understand English—just Urdu.

She shut the window, and then headed back to the bed. She reached for the book and flipped through the pages, not bothering to read the strange story about Ralph Flabbergast again, just looking at the handwriting. When she reached the end of the handwriting, she stopped.

Wasn't that beautiful?

A new line of elegant script flowed at the bottom of the page: *Wasn't that beautiful?*

Like it was talking to her. Like it had seen the moth.

She didn't remember reading that earlier and wondered if she might have missed it. But she didn't see how. This morning she had begun reading a handwritten story about Ralph Flabbergast, fool, believer in magic. And now there was a sentence: *Wasn't that beautiful?*

It gave her a strange feeling—as if those too-far-away walls around her had dropped away completely. Like her bed was a raft floating in space. It wasn't a happy, fun, Elizabeth-Dear-discovers-a-spooky-mystery feeling. It was a creepy this-is-scary-and-where-am-I? feeling.

But when she looked at the page again, the sentence had disappeared. She found that reassuring, although she really shouldn't have. When you think about it.

There was a pen on the side table. Leila picked it up.

The last line of the story was now, *He had seen magic.*

Did I see magic? she asked herself. *No. You imagined the new writing. You're still jet lagged. It wasn't real. . . .*

She stared at the page.

Don't do it, she told herself. But the book was like

the light. She was like the moth. Suddenly, she was compelled to write in the space left by the sentence that had disappeared. Maybe she wanted to be sure that it wouldn't come back.

In the book she wrote, *But the magic Ralph loved was fake. It wasn't real.*

Then she put down the pen, slammed the book shut, and put it on the side table. She turned out the light and sat, perfectly still, in the shadows.

It wasn't real.

She felt those words, pulsing in the book beside her, even with her eyes closed.

It doesn't matter, Leila told herself. I'll put the book back on the shelf in the library in the morning. Then I'll forget all about it.

Which just goes to show you that people have no idea what's going to happen to them.

THE EXQUISITE CORPSE

But the magic Ralph loved was fake. It wasn't real.

"How did you do that?" Ralph asked the man in the hat.

"Do what?" The man smiled, each tooth like a piano

key, as his fingers danced over the walnuts.

"How did you make the pea disappear?"

"Why, magic, young lad." The man leaned down, and placed his lips near Ralph's ear. "You do believe in magic, don't you?"

"Of course," Ralph whispered.

Leaning back, the man narrowed his eyes and looked down his long nose. "Yes," he said slowly, hissing like a thoughtful snake. "Yes, I believe you do. It's not everyone that does, these days."

"Can you teach me?"

"I can do better than that." Reaching into the pocket of his vest, the man brought out a small glass vial with a silver stopper. "I can give you a bit of magic, if you like. Three magics per bottle."

"Wow!" Ralph reached for the vial.

"Not so fast, young man! Something this precious costs money. I can't go giving it away for free."

The silver stopper winked in the sunlight, setting Ralph on fire with wanting. He had to have that bottle. He had to! "How much?" he asked.

The man wrapped his fingers around the bottle and

closed his eyes. "Two paper dollars . . . one half dollar . . . five quarters . . . a dime . . . three nickels . . . forty-seven pennies."

Ralph began to feel very queer. How strange that this man would list exactly the coins that Ralph had hidden behind the loose board at the back of the bread box. All of the money he had earned from doing odd jobs and helping his father at the store for the past two years.

The man's black eyes were open now, and so was his palm. The vial shone like a faint star. Ralph had to have it.

"I'll be right back," Ralph said.

CHAPTER FIVE

Kai

THE MOMENT KAI PUSHED open the door to the kitchen, she was overwhelmed by the smell of apples and cinnamon and something else—ginger?—and she saw herself as a small child, reaching for the stove, and someone bending down to tell her gently, "No, no, Kai, the cake isn't finished yet."

"I've made my famous apple cake for dessert," Lavinia crowed. "It was your daddy's favorite! He drug the recipe out of me when he was in high school."

Kai did not know what to say. Her mother always whispered the words, "your father," as if he were something too special to share with the world. Kai was used to thinking of him as a myth, or maybe a magical creature—not as someone who ate cake. Or baked it. Kai stood for a moment, just breathing. For some reason, she could not imagine the taste. "It smells really good."

"Well, let's eat, then!" Lavinia boomed. "The sooner we get to dinner, the sooner we get to dessert. Go wash up, sugar."

Kai used the small downstairs bathroom, enjoying the fancy soap cut into the shape of a rose and the lace-trimmed towels. Those were the kind of things her mother always said were "too good to use," so they sat in a closet, collecting dust, while they used the same old set of rose-patterned towels that had faded to gray with too many washings. Schuyler was a very careful woman. Very careful and reliable, which was, Kai thought, mostly good. But she was also a woman who knew that good things could be used up too soon, gone before their time, and that fact ruled both her life and Kai's.

Kai walked into the dining room. Lace doilies covered every available surface, and oil paintings of roses covered the walls. The dining table gleamed with old wood and a silver candelabra. Silver sprigs of flowers snaked up and down the faded wallpaper, and the late-afternoon light cast everything in shadow and shades of gold.

Two plates of sausage and sauerkraut were on the table, along with a small salad at each setting. Kai looked at the sauerkraut suspiciously. She did not like sauerkraut.

"Old family recipe," Lavinia said, reading her expression. "You'll like it."

"You promise?" Kai asked doubtfully, but she liked the old lady, so she tried a bite. She paused a moment, chewing.

"See?"

"That's really good."

"Don't I know it. Eat some with a bite of that sausage there."

Kai obeyed, and was rewarded with a burst of savory, sour, sweet deliciousness that crunched and melted across her tongue.

"Your mother called," Lavinia said as Kai took another bite. "She sends her love and says she hopes you've practiced the violin."

Kai chewed thoroughly, then swallowed. "Thanks." Kai thought about her violin, closed in its case, shut in the dark closet. Lavinia didn't ask any more questions, didn't actually ask if she had practiced. And so Kai didn't actually lie.

"How was the Walgreens?" Lavinia asked.

Kai told her great-aunt about Doodle, and Pettyfer, and the moth.

"Oh, she's a hoot, that Doodle Martell!" Lavinia crowed. "Her father's a hoot, too. Poor man."

"Why poor man?"

Lavina looked up at the ceiling and shook her head. "He's got a thankless job, I tell you. Working in that casket factory."

"The Pettyfer factory?" Interesting. Doodle hadn't mentioned that her father worked there.

Lavinia scowled. "That's what folks call it, but the rightful name is American Casket."

"Would it be all right if I go look for this Celestial Moth thing?" Kai asked.

"Why not?" Lavinia asked.

"Well, it's after—dinner." Kai stopped herself from saying "after *dark*," though she cast a glance toward the window behind Lavinia, where long shadows stretched across the garden.

"The moth ain't going to come out during the daytime, is it?" Lavinia asked. "My old uncle used to talk about those moths. Said they liked the Lightning Tree."

"What's that?"

"An old sycamore what got blasted by lightning about a hundred fifty years ago. Seared off a major branch, so that it grew all lopsided for years and years. It's still there, I think."

"Where is it?" Kai couldn't wait to hand over this idea to Doodle.

"Next to the casket factory," Lavinia said, just before shoving a huge bite of salad into her mouth. A little piece of green spinach poked out of the corner of her mouth, which made her look like a happy lizard munching a leaf.

Next to the casket factory? Kai's old habit of worrying about what her mother would think kicked in. Kai had never been allowed outside after dark by herself, and her mother would go ballistic if she knew that she was planning to creep around a dark coffin factory. . . . She felt that fizzy, pent-up, almost-bursting feeling she'd had earlier, when Lavinia had said she could walk to the Walgreens.

Lavinia looked over her shoulder, out the window. "Clear skies," she said. "Sometimes, with heat like this, we get a storm. But you should have a good view of the stars tonight."

The stars. You never could see them very well in

Baltimore, and Kai was seized with the urge to go outside right then. After all, her mother would never have to know. It would be like the violin practice—she just wouldn't mention it. And so what if the factory made caskets? They were just boxes. It was just a factory. It's not like it would be scary. Swallowing her fear along with another bite of sausage, she asked, "Where's the factory?"

Lavinia gestured over her shoulder, toward the window where the light was fading quickly. She winked with her small eye, while the larger one bulged wider. "Right at the other edge of the graveyard, sugar," she said.

After dinner and apple cake (Kai actually ate half the cake—it was that good), Kai went upstairs to her room to grab a sweater when she spotted the book on her bed again. Slowly, as if she were approaching a snake, Kai crept near. She opened the book.

"No way," she whispered.

There was more story.

Kai skimmed the page. A vial? What—what was this?

A knock on the door made Kai jump. "Eee!" she shouted. The book fell to the floor with a thump as the handle turned and . . .

"Jeez, what's the matter, you drink too much coffee, or something?" Doodle asked as she stomped into the room.

Kai crossed over to the door and peered into the deserted hallway. The faint smell of apple cake was all that lingered there. "Who let you in?"

"Lavinia, of course." Doodle looked around. The glow from the setting sun had turned the white walls and coverlet rosy. "I really love this room," she said. "It gets the best light." For a moment, Kai had forgotten that Doodle knew her great-aunt. And, apparently, her house. "What's this?" And before Kai could stop her, Doodle had swooped down and picked up *The Exquisite Corpse*.

Kai snatched it away.

"Whoa!" Doodle said. "What is it, your diary or something?"

"No, it's . . ." But Kai didn't know how to finish the sentence. *It's a freaky magic book*? "Yeah, it's kind of my diary."

Doodle just shrugged. "Cool. So, you want to go look for a moth?" she asked. She held up an orange-handled, battered butterfly net.

"Sure." The two girls headed downstairs and into the kitchen to say good-bye to Kai's great-aunt. Lavinia sat at a well-worn farm table, scribbling madly on a yellow legal pad. She looked up and nodded at Doodle's net. "You girls fixing to go get yourselves a moth? You ain't hoping to catch it with that, are you?"

Now, it was true that this net had been purchased at Target for a dollar. And it was true that it did, perhaps, have a hole in it. "Don't you think it's big enough?" Doodle asked.

"Too large, if you ask me." Lavinia chewed her lip. She hauled herself up from the table and stomped across the room to yank open a closet door. Out spilled a mountain of things: hockey gear, three umbrellas, a beach ball (inflated), a goblet made of golden plastic, a stuffed bear, a pith helmet, several pairs of shoes, and a lampshade rolled around her feet. She thrust her arm into the mass of stuff, and after a moment of banging and rattling, she pulled out a long ivory handle, at the end of which was a silver net that glittered in the low lamplight. "There's what you'll need!"

"We couldn't possibly take that," Kai said. The

beautiful net looked as if it belonged in a museum.

"Why not?" Lavinia demanded. "You're only borrowing it. This belonged to *my* great-aunt!"

"We'll bring it right back," Doodle promised.

"All right, girls, happy hunting!" Lavinia boomed. "Don't let me keep you!" Kai and Doodle swirled in Lavinia's eddy as she circled them, herding them toward the back door. Before she knew what was happening, Kai found herself standing on the vine-covered porch.

"Good night!" Lavinia shut the door.

The girls blinked at the closed door for a moment.

Kai turned to Doodle, who was now staring at the beautiful net. "Was that a little weird?" Kai asked.

"Poets are like that, sometimes," Doodle told her. "Now, let's go catch a moth."

The night was a revelation for Kai. It would be an exaggeration to say that she had never been outside at night, but it would not be a *huge* exaggeration. She had certainly never been outside at night without an adult. She had never been allowed to roam about the neighborhood once darkness fell, and now it was as if she were full of helium, like she might float away at any moment, right up to the stars. Her fingers brushed the trunk of a tree as she walked past, feeling the rough, ridged bumps and the smooth moss.

"What are you doing?" Doodle asked.

"Just . . . just feeling the bark." It had looked different in the dark. Although everything looked different in the dim light, Kai was surprised at how much she was able to see, and she found herself noticing things she had not paid attention to before. She and Doodle each had a flashlight, but the beams only illuminated a small patch of ground before their feet. It made the darkness around them seem blacker, somehow. Kai had never before realized that there are a thousand shades of shadow between gray and black.

The moon was not full, but it hung low, fat and yellow, looking close enough to step onto. It seemed like a different moon entirely from the sick, pale thumbnail that she often glimpsed through her bedroom window back home. "The moon is huge here," Kai said.

"It'll get smaller as the night goes on." A twig snapped beneath Doodle's foot. "When it's higher in the sky."

"Because it's getting farther away?"

"No—it's called the moon illusion. When it's low on the horizon, you see it next to trees and telephone poles, and stuff, so it looks bigger. When it's up in the sky, there's no—" Doodle's feet kept moving, but her words stopped.

"Comparison?"

"Yeah. When it's by itself, you can't tell how huge it really is."

Now that the sun had set, everything seemed to breathe again. Around Kai, insects chirped. She tried to follow the tune. It reminded her of something—the opening bars of a Haydn sonata, maybe? The digits of her left hand tapped against her thigh, remembering the fingering of the opening bars. She didn't even notice herself doing it, but I did, and that meant she was concentrating on the strangeness around her.

A white cat darted across a yard. A small light flickered. Then another. "Fireflies!"

"We could catch some, if you want," Doodle said.

"No, that's okay." Kai hadn't meant to sound so excited, but the flashes had taken her by surprise. She just had never seen lightning bugs in real life before, and it made her both happy and a little sad as she wondered how long it had been since her mother had seen one. "How are we going to find these moth things?"

"They're bioluminescent. Like the fireflies, only not as bright." Doodle took a sharp turn, and Kai nearly danced after her, swinging her great-aunt's silver net. Over on the other side of the iron fence, gravestones hulked, casting long, eerie shadows. "Here we are," Doodle said.

Well, now that they were *here*, Kai did not like the look of the place very much. But she didn't want to say that to Doodle. "What's that?" she asked, pointing to the building hulking on the far side of the fence.

"American Casket, of course. Home of the famous Eternal Casket. Guaranteed to stay in perfect shape for two hundred years."

"Wow," Kai said. "How would anyone know?"

"Exactly," Doodle replied.

"So—uh, what now?"

"We go inside." Doodle had already slipped through the gate, which—though chained—gaped wide enough to let a middle schooler through.

Now, as I've already mentioned, Kai was a planner. But in all of Kai's years of planning, she had never before come up with a strategy for what to do if a friend headed into a creepy-looking graveyard, expecting her to follow. Kai was not someone who was very accustomed to being brave. In fact, the bravest thing Kai'd ever had to do was perform Mozart's Concerto #4 in D Major for Susan Laviere, which was terrifying, but in a completely different way. So you will please excuse her for thinking that it might be wise to just leave Doodle in the graveyard and head on home, preferably at top speed.

But she only thought that for a moment. Then she realized what a lowdown thing it would be to let a friend go into a graveyard full of hunching, hulking white stones all alone after dark. And so she forced one foot in front of the other.

Kai followed an elegant stone footpath, and shuddered as the wind blew behind her, making the gate creak like it thought it was a gate from some scary movie. "Doodle?" she called, as she wound her way between massive headstones. A white marble woman looked up at the sky, rooted to a pedestal that read, *M. Jonas 1835–1913.*

She tried not to think of M. Jonas under the ground, waiting to reach up and grab at her ankles. She called again.

"Over here!" Doodle cried.

Kai spotted her nearby, leaning over, looking at something at the base of a large tree. The tree was hunched and twisted, with a cluster of branches on one side that seemed to reach for the marble statue. This was clearly the Lightning Tree. Kai forgot her fear and hurried to join her. "Did you find one?"

"Look." Doodle's voice was a whisper. She pointed at the trunk.

Kai clicked on her flashlight, but Doodle snapped, "Turn it off." Kai did.

"I don't see anything."

"Wait."

So she did. Kai stared at the trunk of the tree, where Doodle pointed to a black hollow. Kai stood on tiptoe, looking down into the darkness. Slowly, something began to appear. Something long and luminous, like a misshapen pearl, glowed faint blue. "That's not a moth. Is it?"

"No, but it could be a cocoon." Delicately, Doodle plucked it from the bark. "It's covered in resin."

"Like a bug in amber?" Kai had seen a display of prehistoric insects at the natural history museum.

"Exactly."

Doodle shone her flashlight on a red flower growing near the base of the tree. "Hm, I've seen this flower before. There's a bunch of them that grow in a field close by. But the factory always mows it." She peered again at the cocoon.

Kai was just about to ask if Doodle thought it was a cocoon for a Celestial Moth, when a loud crack snapped behind them. Kai wheeled; Doodle leaped to her feet.

Something flashed—a movement between the gravestones. Kai let out a little scream.

Doodle lifted her eyebrows. "Really? You're screaming?"

Kai couldn't catch her breath. She wanted to say, "Something's there!" but she couldn't make the words come out. Not that it mattered. The thing moved again, and Doodle started chasing it.

"Don't leave me!" Kai called, running after her friend, who was pounding up the footpath.

The thing was on the other side of the iron gate, near the side of the coffin factory. At the sound of Doodle's footsteps, the thing raced off.

Oh, thank god, Kai thought, immediately followed

by—*Why did Lavinia let me out after dark? Why?* "Stop!" Doodle shouted. "Stop, you stupid jerk!" She dashed after the thing, but it had disappeared around the corner of the building. She shook the net angrily in the general direction of the escapee.

"What was that?" Kai asked.

"Not what," Doodle said, "who."

Doodle looked in her net. The cocoon was still there, unharmed. She looked over at Kai. "Come on," she said.

Kai didn't know what to make of any of this. "What was that all about?"

Doodle stormed ahead like a hurricane. She didn't stop; she didn't slow down. She only spoke one word. "Pettyfer," she said.

The pale blue pearl in the net receded as Doodle stomped on. Kai wondered if it really was a cocoon.

And, if so, she wondered what was inside.

THE EXQUISITE CORPSE

What was inside? *Ralph peered at the vial. It was small and flat, made of smoky purple glass. The man had told him to open it only when he was alone. There are three magics inside, he had said. Don't let them all out at once.*

Ralph hurried toward home, but he did not make it all the way. He passed American Casket and walked through a field of bright red flowers. Halfway across, he looked up at the sky, which was bleached close to white by the harsh sun. Around him, there were no sounds but the music of the grasshoppers at his feet. He stood in the shade of a slender sycamore and pressed his back against the patchy gray-and-white bark. Carefully, he unscrewed the silver cap on his vial. Like mist, fine white powder rose from the vial and a light breeze blew it against the tree. Ralph peered up at the canopy of wide, seven pointed green leaves, wondering for a moment if he was like Jack and the Beanstalk, and if the tree might rise into the bleached sky.

The grasshoppers whirred on. Nothing happened.

Perhaps I need to make a wish, *Ralph thought.* "I wish," *Ralph said aloud,* "that something would happen."

Above him, the leaves whispered for a moment, and then were still.

Ralph fought the urge to dump out all of the powder in the vial. Be patient, *Ralph told himself.* Even Jack's beanstalk didn't grow right away. *He screwed the cap* back onto the vial and hurried home.

The smell of cabbage overwhelmed him the moment he walked into the kitchen. As usual, his mother was at the stove, stirring. Ralph and his entire family stank of sauerkraut. All of their clothes stank of sauerkraut. That's because Ralph's mother put sauerkraut on everything. His parents were even starting to sell it at the store. It was his great-grandmother's secret recipe, and she said that it was what had helped her live to the age of 103. Sometimes Ralph wondered if he wanted to be a stinky, sauerkrauty 103-year-old, but he never said so to his mother, as it would have broken her heart.

"Where've you been?" Ralph's mother asked the moment he banged open the door.

"In town," Ralph said. His hand automatically went to the vial in his pocket, and he closed his fingers around it.

"What've you got there?" Mrs. Flabbergast planted her fists on her wide hips.

"Nothing." Ralph blushed as red as a boiled lobster.

"Ralph . . ."

"It's nothing, really," Ralph said, pulling the vial out of his pocket and holding it out to his mother. "It's just . . . um . . ."

"Looks like a fancy salt shaker."

"It is! Yes! I found it." Ralph did not have much practice lying, and it showed.

"Hm." Then, to Ralph's horror, Mrs. Flabbergast opened the vial and shook a bit of the white powder into the sauerkraut cabbage. "Well, I hope this does something for the sauerkraut," she said. Then she handed the vial back to Ralph, whose jaw dangled dangerously close to the floor.

That evening, a storm blew in around dinnertime. Lightning flashed; thunder boomed. Nobody in the Flabbergast family noticed. They were too busy devouring sauerkraut, which—everyone agreed—was (for once) scrumptious.

Almost magically so.

CHAPTER SIX
Leila

THE MORNING SUN ROSE feebly through the smoky Lahore sky. Leila was still jet lagged, and was only now—too late—beginning to feel tired after a sleepless night, but she didn't go back to bed. She had not dared to step out into the hallway until the sun rose. Elizabeth and Jennifer Dear often discovered mysteries when roaming around in strange, dark houses, but Leila felt she had enough mysteries already. For example: what was the deal with this freaky book? That was pretty much number one. That and, who was making up new parts to this story? What did sauerkraut have to do with anything? Was someone just messing with her?

Leila padded into the library and pushed *The Exquisite Corpse* back into the lone empty space on the shelf.

Her body loosened the moment she turned her back and walked out of the library. Now she could get a little nap before breakfast.

Back in her room, Leila slipped between the soft white sheets and closed her eyes. She did not bother closing the blinds. Leila liked sleeping with the sun on her face. It made her feel like a cat. Thinking of Steve's gray tail, she curled her knees toward her chest. Some pinchy pointy thing dug into her thigh.

"Ow!" Leila felt for the object and pulled out a book. Then she let out a slight shriek and fell out of bed.

I don't even have to tell you, do I? Fine, I will. It was *The Exquisite Corpse.*

She stood up and limped to the door, then down the hall. She peeked into the library. There was an empty space on the shelf where the book should be.

Leila knew that she was not dreaming, but she truly wished she were. She had always longed to have a strange, magical adventure. It sounded great when it happened in books! But now that she *was* having a strange adventure, she wished she could just go home. Well, maybe not home. Not yet. She just wanted to go somewhere nonmagical.

Someplace comfortable. Someplace where the books did not follow one around.

After all, she realized, this book situation wouldn't even make a good blog. People would just think she was crazypants. That her brain had gone soft in the heat.

Well! Leila certainly was not about to go back to her room, so she headed downstairs to the kitchen.

The kitchen was an interesting place. For one thing, there were two kitchens. "One for show, and one for blow," as her mother would say. There was a beautiful kitchen with granite countertops and knives in a rack. It had a lovely white wooden table and matching chairs, and had a window that looked out onto a mango tree. Along one wall of the kitchen was a door. This door led to the second kitchen: the *real* kitchen. This was a cramped, narrow place with a concrete floor and pots and pans that looked like they had been used to bash rocks. This was where the servants cooked the meals. The show kitchen was for the family to make toast or heat up something in the microwave.

Leila sat down in a white wooden chair for a moment. Then she decided that she should drink a glass of water.

Elizabeth Dear always drank water when she needed to calm down. She crossed to the cabinets and pulled one open. Bowls. She tried the next one and let out a little yelp.

Can you guess what was inside?

"No," she whispered, even as she pulled out *The Exquisite Corpse*. She flipped the pages. It was the same book. There was no doubt about it. It was the same. The same handwriting.

She clutched the book to her chest, thinking about how to destroy it.

There was no point in throwing it away, after all. It would just creep up on her again, like a book boomerang. What else? What else could she do?

Her eye fell on the stove. It was gas.

I'll burn it, Leila thought. Hah!

The right burner lit with a whoosh, and she held the book over the flame, letting fire lick at the edge of a page. The paper flared and the whole book burst into flame. Leila let out a little squeal, and let go. The pages sat awkwardly on the burner, blazing. "Sorry, sorry," Leila whispered as she watched it burn. Seized with a sudden panic that the fire might burn down the whole house, Leila grabbed a pair of metal tongs hanging beside the stove and used them to grab the book. She tossed it into the sink.

Thick black smoke had started to fill the kitchen, smelling like the hippie gift shop that her friend Ta'Mara loved. Leila coughed and wondered if there was a fire extinguisher—

Footsteps slammed toward the kitchen, and Leila thought about running, but Samir appeared before she could take off. "Is the house on fire?" he cried.

"It's not the—ugh!" Coughing, Leila fanned the smoke away from her face. "It's not the house!" She turned on the tap, dousing the pages while Samir slapped on the fan beneath the microwave. Then he cranked open the window.

A fire alarm started to shriek. It was directly over Leila's head, and seemed to be screaming inside her skull. "Do something!"

"*Chup kar!*" Samir grabbed a broom and gave the alarm a solid whack, knocking it to the floor, where it died with a squawk. He looked up at Leila. "I did not even know we had that thing."

Gingerly, Leila pulled her hands away from her ears.

The smoke had finally died down, and Leila turned off the tap. The book lay in the sink, soggy, but otherwise undamaged.

"Oh," Leila whispered. She picked up the book.

It hadn't burned. She opened it. The ink hadn't run under the water.

In fact, there was a new sentence: *You couldn't see the damage that the fire had caused, but it was there.*

She slammed it shut.

"What's that?" Samir asked, looking at the wet book. Then he looked at Leila's face. "Are you all right? You look—"

"What's going on?" Babar Taya burst into the kitchen, followed by his wife and a very irritated-looking Rabeea. Everyone was in their pajamas, but Jamila Tai had pulled a jacket on over her sleepwear. "Is everyone all right?"

Wali pranced in shouting, "What was that? *Kya ho raha hai?* What is the smell?"

A drop of water dripped from the book onto Leila's little toe.

"Leila just burned some toast," Samir explained. "Did you know that we had a—" He gestured to the smoke detector. "Did you know that it works?"

"It doesn't look like it works anymore," Rabeea said, eyeing the smashed pieces on the floor.

"Of course we have a smoke detector," Jamila Tai put in. "I had Chirragh install it."

"Why?" Rabeea asked. "The house is concrete."

"Because your father and I lived in Connecticut for two years, and everyone in the United States has a fire alarm," Jamila Tai replied. "They're positively pathological about reminding you to check the batteries—I never broke the habit. Leila, if you would like some toast, I'd be happy to make you some."

Leila glanced at Samir. His permanently cocked eyebrow lifted slightly, and he nodded.

"Yes," she said slowly, sinking into a chair. "Thank you so much."

"I'm going back to bed," Rabeea announced. Nobody tried to stop her.

Wali climbed into the chair beside hers. "Halvah poori!" As usual, everyone ignored him as they bustled around. Babar Taya began measuring coffee and Jamila Tai asked if anyone else was in the mood for roti. Then she shouted for Chirragh, who limped in wearing his signature glare.

Silently, Samir placed a glass of orange juice in front of Leila. She looked up at him, and he smiled gently. The damp book sat in her lap, and Samir glanced down at it. He didn't mention it.

You couldn't see the damage that the fire had caused, but it was there.

The sentence was burned into Leila's mind. She tightened her grip on the book.

It had only just dawned on her to wonder what the book might want from her.

After lunch, Jamila Tai had asked Leila if she wanted to buy any trinkets—that's how she put it, "trinkets"—for friends or family while she was visiting Pakistan. Nadia had asked for purple *khusas*, size 5, and Leila wanted some bangles for Ta'Mara, so she said yes. Rabeea announced that she wanted to get some kohl for her eyes, and Wali liked any excuse to leave the house, so he asked if he could come along.

So they all piled into the car, and Asif, the driver, pulled into traffic. "I can't find my seat belt," Leila said, wondering if Rabeea was sitting on it. They were squashed into the backseat with Jamila Tai.

"Oh, I don't think we have them in this car," Jamila Tai said vaguely.

Wali was in the front passenger seat, playing with the radio and bouncing happily.

Leila's parents were heavily into seat belts and life vests and bike helmets. Most of that stuff was required by law, anyway. But Leila had noticed that people in Pakistan didn't seem as . . . safety conscious . . . as Americans. She was noticing it now, as Asif's driving technique seemed to be to head straight for all oncoming cars at top speed until the last moment, and then swerve aside while honking furiously. Nobody else seemed to think that this technique needed improvement. Leila shut her eyes and focused on her breathing. It was something her mother liked to do when she was stressed out. When she inhaled, she smelled the smoke that lingered in her hair from that morning's book disaster. Leila inhaled again, hoping that the book wouldn't decide to follow her on the shopping trip. For some reason, this relaxation technique was not working.

They pulled into a parking lot in front of what appeared to be a strip mall. But it wasn't like an American strip mall; it was crammed with stores, each of which was overflowing with goods. An old man with one hand used his stump to bang on the car window. His black eyes pleaded as he said something in Urdu, the words muffled through the glass window. Leila shrank back a moment as a memory surfaced—she was a little girl, visiting her grandmother in Lahore. A despairing woman held a black-eyed baby up to the car window, and Leila had buried her face in her grandmother's shawl and burst into tears. For years, Leila had remembered Lahore as a place where she was treated like a princess. She had forgotten what it was like to be out in the city.

Leila reached for her purse, but Rabeea put her hand on Leila's wrist. "They will all come over," Rabeea told her. Her eyes were gentle, but her voice was firm. That was when Leila realized that people were milling around the cars—children selling flowers, old women, crippled, poor, desperate people.

"Sad." It was the only word Leila could think of. All

other sentences had been squeezed from her—her throat was closed, her chest heaved with the weight of sadness so strong that it felt like fear.

"You can't help them all," Rabeea said. "Besides, a lot of them work for organized crime. The bosses take the money and let the people starve."

Leila wasn't sure if that was supposed to make her feel better, but it didn't. Instead, she felt as if she had been stabbed—unable to move with the shock. She was starting to wonder if Rabeea's heart was made of granite.

Jamila Tai stared straight ahead as Wali pointed to a vendor who stood with an enormous bouquet of gaudy balloons.

Leila looked down at her lap. Breathe in, she told herself. Breathe out.

Beyond the vendor was the market. Shop after shop—fashionable children's clothes, glittering jewels, a bank, a carpet store with vibrant rugs. Asif wove through the parking lot and jerked to a stop. Lightly, he sprang from the driver's seat and yanked open Leila's door.

"Thanks," Leila told him. *"Shukria."*

"You are welcare." He enunciated, smiling beneath his

black mustache. Asif was a young guy, only in his twenties, and very handsome. Leila had seen him helping out with the kitchen work once or twice. He usually had earphones plugged into his ears, and would chat on the phone while arranging fruit on a platter. She wondered what his life would be like in the United States.

"Liberty Market," Jamila Tai announced, as if she were a stewardess. She led Leila to the bangle stall and Wali stood on tiptoe to help her choose. Leila was pretty sure that Ta'Mara's favorite color was purple, but Wali insisted that turquoise was the nicest, so that's what Leila chose. Then the jewelry seller—a pockmarked man with large ears and several missing teeth—tried to interest her in some earrings. He held them up to his own ears, as if he were a model. Leila had to mash her lips together to keep herself from giggling. For a moment, she considered getting them for Aimee, but rejected the idea just as quickly. What would be the point? "Just these," Leila said, gesturing to the turquoise bangles.

They went to a store that sold CDs and DVDs—all pirated, and offered for a fraction of the price that they would cost in the United States.

"*Pakistan Idol!*" Wali cried, pointing to a rack of CDs. "Zamad Baig!"

"He won the first season," Rabeea explained. "Wali is his biggest fan."

"Nooo," Wali singsonged. "I wanted the other one to win."

"Muhammad Shoaib," Jamila Tai said. "Samir favored him, too."

Rabeea smiled, clearly embarrassed. "It's my mom's favorite show."

"And yours!" Wali chirped, as Rabeea glared.

"It's *my* mom's favorite, too," Leila said. "I mean, *American Idol* is. I don't know if she knows about *Pakistan Idol*." It seemed funny and strange to see *Pakistan Idol* written out in the same text used for the show in the United States, just as it was strange to see a Spider-Man balloon for sale beside a man selling mangoes from a donkey cart. For Leila, Pakistan was a jumble of the familiar and unfamiliar, which made every moment seem like a dream.

Leila bought a copy of the *Pakistan Idol* CD for her mom. Then Rabeea announced that she wanted to get her eyebrows threaded. Jamila Tai wanted to get her hair blown out and set. "What would you like, Leila?" she asked. "Would you like to have your nails painted?"

"Oh, no, thank you." Leila's friends were into nail polish, but Leila thought it made her fingers feel weird and heavy.

"I don't want to go to the beauty parlor!" Wali whined.

Jamila Tai was about to insist that Leila come, but Leila offered to take Wali to get ice cream, instead. This was met with a response from Wali that was so enthusiastic as to be irresistible.

"He'll just drive us crazy if he stays with us, anyway," Rabeea said, already heading up the steps to the salon.

Jamila Tai frowned, but in the end, she had to agree. There was an ice-cream place only three doors down from the beauty parlor. She didn't need to point it out. Wali knew the way.

As Jamila Tai and Rabeea disappeared behind the frosted glass door, Leila felt happy, and almost triumphant. She was in a foreign country, and she was taking her little cousin for ice cream. This felt *very* Elizabeth Dear. "What's your favorite flavor?" she asked Wali.

"Vanilla!" he said, which made her laugh. "Is vanilla wrong?" he asked.

"Absolutely not," Leila told him. "Vanilla's great. Classic."

Ahead of them, a boy walked down the street leading two goats. One was white, except for a long red stripe down his back, and a red marking on his right flank in the shape of a flower. The other was black. Both goats wore garlands of flowers on their horns and around their necks. They were the fanciest goats Leila had ever seen.

"Wow!" Leila said, reaching for her camera.

"They are for Eid," Wali explained as Leila snapped a photo.

The boy leading the goats looked questioningly at Leila. She gave the boy a thumbs-up.

He said something to her in Punjabi, so she smiled and said, "Nice goat!" Then she gave him another thumbs-up.

The boy said something else.

"He wants to know if you want to see them more closely," Wali explained. "They are both female."

"Oh, sure!" Leila replied, nodding. Another thumbs-up. She had never used this gesture before, but it seemed like the only appropriate response to this particular situation.

The boy led over the goats, and she took some more photos. The white one tried to nibble the end of her scarf, which made Leila laugh. She scolded her, and petted her neck. "Who's a good goat?" she asked. "Who's a sweetie goat? Hm?" The goat butted at her, and she kissed her head. "Oh, I just want to take her home with me!"

The goatherd looked at Wali, who said something in Punjabi and gestured to Leila. She assumed he had translated what she said as the goatherd showed off the goats, opening their mouths and showing their teeth and everything. Leila could see that he was really proud of his goats. She nodded and smiled and petted them some more.

"He wants to know which one you like the best," Wali said.

"I like them both," Leila said. "Well, I guess the white one. She has personality." She patted the white one again. "And I love the henna job."

Wali and the goatherd exchanged a few words. Then the goat boy bowed low to Leila, and she gave him another smile. The goatherd said something else in Punjabi.

"He wants five hundred rupees now," Wali said.

"What? What for?"

"The goat," Wali explained, as if it was perfectly obvious.

Leila's happy feeling dried up. She had heard of beggars like this—who demanded money when someone took their photo. She was about to refuse, but when she looked down, she saw that the boy had no shoes, only thick calluses on dusty feet. She felt a deep sense of shame.

Maybe I can't help them all, Leila thought, remembering Rabeea's words. But I can help this boy with the goats. He's walking around, hoping people will photograph his fancy goat. That's insane. I'm probably the only customer he'll have all day. All *week*. It wasn't like Lahore was crawling with tourists.

Leila dug around in her pocket and pulled out five hundred rupees. She wasn't really sure how much real money that was. How many dollars. It took a ton of rupees to make one dollar, she knew that much. The goatherd smiled and said shukria.

"Shukria," she said back to him, and he smiled again.

"That's a great goat!" Wali said in excitement, which made her laugh.

Well, he had a point. The goat was pretty cute.

Leila scrolled through the photos of the goat on her camera. They came out really well. There was one where it looked like the goat was smiling, giving her a knowing look. She couldn't wait to show Ta'Mara. She would think it was hilarious. Which it was.

Fancy goats.

Hah!

Even the goats get dressed up for Eid here, Leila thought, smiling, and was immediately distracted by Wali, who had spotted the man selling Spider-Man balloons. Leila didn't have time to wonder how soon the Eid holiday was, or what the goats had to do with it.

Ice cream does not take long to eat, unless you are seven and lapping up tiny licks in order to make the treat last longer. Leila didn't mind, even though she had finished her ice cream long ago. She was enjoying sitting with Wali, scrolling through her photos, looking at the goat. She was enjoying not being home with that creepy book, and hardly even thinking about it, except for once in a while. But even then, it didn't seem as scary as it had that morning. In fact, Leila was beginning to believe she had imagined the whole thing. Jet lag can explain a great deal.

The ice-cream place was clean and bright, and could have been located in any mall in the United States. Leila felt comfortable there. Well, she felt comfortable until a handsome boy with mischievous hair walked in.

"Leila!" Zain cried, as if Leila were the very person he had been hoping to see. He wore a cream salwar kameez, and looked thoroughly handsome as he walked over to their table and mussed Wali's hair.

"Hey!" Wali griped. He didn't look up from his ice cream.

"I should have known I'd find you here," Zain said as he leaned against the marble table. "It's the best ice cream in Lahore."

Leila smiled, hoping that her skin was aglow from the embarrassment she was feeling. Elizabeth Dear always managed to make blushing seem charming. She wondered if she should ask after Zain's mother, the way Elizabeth would have, or if that would seem weird.

"What flavor did you have?" Zain asked her. "My mother always wants coffee. Two pints of coffee, one of chocolate chip. The chocolate chip is for me."

With a smile, he stepped up to the counter and placed his order. She watched him as he waited, leaning against the marble counter. By the time Zain's order arrived, Wali was finished, so he and Leila joined Zain on his way out the door.

He started toward a white Lexus, then turned to grin at Leila. "Maybe this won't arrive at its destination," Zain said, holding up the bag. Leila was about to reply, when a man tugged at Zain's elbow. The man was very small, only a head taller than Wali, and his face was a web of deep wrinkles spun across dark skin. He wore a pointed cap wrapped with tinsel, and what looked like a filthy orange sheet. He said something to Zain and looked at Leila.

"What?" Leila said.

Zain shook him off and replied angrily. But the man continued to stare at Leila from the shade of his thick gray eyebrows. His gaze held her paralyzed, and he said something to her slowly, as if he could make her understand. But she didn't understand.

The man reached toward her, but Leila felt unable to duck away. His fingers touched the top of her head.

Leila finally found her voice. "What's he doing?"

"He is a fakir," Wali explained as Zain pulled out his wallet. "He gives you a blessing."

Leila didn't find this terribly comforting, but at last the fakir stopped speaking. Zain offered the man a bill, but the fakir's nostrils flared in disgust. Still, he took the money before walking away.

"I apologize." Zain folded his wallet and placed it back in his breast pocket. "There are beggars everywhere. It's getting so bad."

"He's a holy man." Wali spoke to Leila, ignored Zain.

"What did he say?" Leila asked.

"He said that the world is a miracle," Wali explained. "He said that you should not fear the world, but should look to the book for answers."

"The book?" Leila repeated. Her head felt a little bit spinny. How could the fakir know about—

"The Quran, I presume," Zain put in.

Leila asked herself what Elizabeth Dear would do, but she did not manage to come up with an answer. This was all getting too peculiar. Was the fakir talking about the Quran, or about *her* book? Her magic book? The one that seemed to be writing its own story every time she shut the pages? *But he couldn't be, because that book is not magic.*

She looked over at Zain, who was smiling at her, as if he hoped to comfort her. *That's what's real,* she told herself. *This is my story. I get to decide on my story, and my story is a romantic adventure! Because I lead a life of international travel and excitement!*

This, my friends, is known as wishful thinking.

THE EXQUISITE CORPSE

You could not see the damage the fire had caused, but it was there.

There were many stories about why fire had not destroyed the house. Some said that it was made of stone, and fire could not burn it. Some said that a sudden rainstorm had put out the fire while it was still burning. And some said that it was impossible to burn a house made cold by the heart of Melchisedec Jonas.

Let me tell you about him.

Melchisedec Jonas spent eight years as the foreman at American Casket Company.

"He's the best foreman I've ever had," his boss, Mr.

Pickle, would say as he slapped Melchisedec on the back. Of course, Melchisedec was the only foreman he'd ever had. It didn't matter.

Melchisedec was tough, and when he was on the line, the caskets were always perfect. Anything less would be torn apart and tossed into the rubbish bin. But folks said that he cared more for the dead than the living—that was how badly he treated the workers. There were no breaks. There was no sympathy. There was only work.

But the factory flourished. And when the factory's owner and his wife died in a mysterious fire, few people were surprised to hear that Melchisedec was to serve as the president of American Casket Company until the owners' oldest child, Edwina, should come of age. Folks were also not surprised to hear that Edwina Pickle and her little brother, Parker, were to be cared for by their new guardian, Melchisedec Jonas. Mr. Pickle always had trusted him.

But Ralph did not know this as he waited patiently in Melchisedec's yard. His parents had been called to Mr. Jonas's house for a meeting. Ralph was now thirteen years old, for five years had passed since Mrs. Flabbergast sprinkled the powder from the vial into her pot of cabbage.

Since that night, all sauerkraut made in the pot had tasted stunningly delicious. Ralph's father began selling Flabbergast's Famous Kraut, and they simply could not keep it on the shelf. For once, Ralph's family was able to save a bit of money.

Now, Melchisedec Jonas wanted to buy the factory, even though there was no factory. He wanted the name, and he wanted the recipe, and he wasn't taking no for an answer.

"Pick a card, any card," Ralph said to the wide-eyed girl who sat across from him. She was shy, with long dark hair and eyes that looked like a deep ocean on a stormy day—blue and green and gray.

"I don't like tricks," the girl said.

"I'll take one!" Her brother grabbed a card. He was taller and livelier than his sister, though he was younger, but not by much.

"Don't show it to me," Ralph told him. He had the little boy put it back in the deck, and amazed him by pulling it from behind the boy's ear.

"Edwina!" the boy squealed with a grin. "Look, it's magic!"

"It's just a trick, Parker," she said. "That's not real magic."

"How do you know?" Ralph asked.

Edwina looked him dead in the eye. "Because I know what real magic looks like."

Ralph's head felt light. "Do you?" he said, holding her gaze. He thought of his vial, which he had hidden in his pocket. He had not opened it in five years.

Not since the day he sprinkled some powder on the tree, and several hours later, it was hit by lightning but did not die. (In fact, the weeks that followed, it sprouted leaves more lush than ever before.) The same day his mother had sprinkled some into the sauerkraut pot, and changed their lives. Two wishes were gone already, thoughtlessly, and Ralph did not dare to use the third.

Ralph believed in real magic, too, and he longed for it, although it frightened him. This was why he learned tricks and kept the vial in his pocket—he wanted to come as close to magic as he could, without actually touching it. He didn't want to waste his last bit of it, and he didn't want to let it out of his sight.

Ralph tried to read what Edwina was thinking of, to

see what was hidden in the depths of those eyes.

The door opened and three adults stormed in.

"Ralph, we're leaving," Mr. Flabbergast announced, holding his hat over his wide belly.

"I'll have my lawyer send you the papers." Melchisedec Jonas was a small man, extravagantly groomed with pale hair slicked to his head and eyes that seemed flat and dead.

Ralph's parents were always polite, but they did not look at Mr. Jonas as they collared Ralph and marched him out the door. And, in this way, Melchisedec Jonas killed the small magic that had almost changed the fortunes of the Flabbergasts.

Mrs. Flabbergast never made another jar of sauerkraut again.

CHAPTER SEVEN

Kai

The library is doing a wonderful job of impersonating a small wooden cottage, Kai thought. It didn't look like the libraries in Baltimore. It didn't look official at all. In fact, if it weren't for the hand-painted sign on the white fence, she never would have cast a second glance at the one-story structure on the main street.

"Why aren't we just looking up the moth on your dad's computer?" Kai asked.

"This library has some stuff you can't get anywhere else," Doodle told her.

Kai lifted her eyebrows at the little old building. "Like dust mites?"

Doodle ignored her, pushing the gate, which yielded with a welcoming creak. The paint on the wooden steps and front porch had been rubbed off by years of people carrying books back and forth. All in all, there was something about the building that made Kai think of a friendly old woman, the kind who loves visitors.

"Doodle!" The young man behind the library counter looked delighted to see her. Colorful tattoos ran up his arms, creeping beneath the turned-up sleeves of a vintage gas-station attendant shirt with *Vinnie* written over the pocket. The sides of his dark hair were cropped close, ending in a bouffant that towered over a pair of black-framed glasses. "Wait there!" he said, ducking behind the counter.

"Who's that?" Kai whispered.

"The librarian, who do you think?" Doodle said back. She did not whisper. Subtlety was not Doodle's strength. "Carlos."

"His name isn't Vinnie?"

Doodle chuckled. "Don't believe everything you read."

Carlos resurfaced holding an enormous, battered volume. "Dug it out of the archives!"

"You're kidding!" Doodle rushed over.

A very thin blonde woman with green eyes and a wide mouth shushed them.

Carlos lowered his voice to a whisper. "It was down there—hi"—Carlos glanced at Kai—"buried in the back. Completely *mis*-filed!" He said this like a man who had endured a great deal of incompetence.

Doodle reached for the book, then held back. "May I?" she asked.

Carlos handed her a pair of white cotton gloves, and she pulled them on.

"Are you going to look at it, or operate on it?" Kai asked.

"Carlos, welcome to Kai." Doodle did not look up as she gently, gently turned the brittle pages of handwritten notes.

"Are you a lepidopterist, too?" Carlos whispered, and shoved his thick glasses up onto the bridge of his nose. They promptly slid down again.

"No, why? Is *everyone* in this town into moths, or something?" Kai asked.

Doodle looked up from the book. Both she and Carlos stared at Kai.

"What?" Kai asked.

"Whittier Springs used to be a huge tourist destination," Doodle explained. "Because of the annual moth migration."

"Tourists?" Kai repeated, smiling a little. She assumed they were pulling her leg.

"We had a unique colony of Celestial Moths; the only one in the country," Carlos explained. "That's why we have the annual festival." He pointed downward. Taped onto the front of the counter was a flyer proclaiming *134th Annual Lepidoptery Fair!*

Yep. He was serious.

Kai felt her face burn hot out to the tips of her eyelashes.

"A hundred years ago, people believed the moths could cure illnesses," Doodle went on. "Even mental ones."

"Yeah, but—" Kai squinched up her nose, face still burning. "You guys don't believe that, right?"

Carlos frowned so hard that his glasses nearly fell off the end of his nose. "How do we know?" he demanded, slowly adjusting his glasses. "Lots of herbs and insects are the basis for modern medicine." Kai didn't really know what to say to this. Carlos had a good point, but Kai wasn't used to being wrong, and she didn't like it much.

"How would a moth cure mental illness?" Kai shot back. "Would it land on your head?"

The lady at the nearby library table shushed them again.

"I apologize," Carlos said to her. His voice was sincere, but the woman frowned. To Kai, he said, "I think the answer to your question is pretty obvious, if you bother to think about it."

Another point for Carlos, which made Kai feel like crawling under the carpet. Since nobody seemed to want to tell her she was right, she decided to drop the subject. "Oh," she said. "Uh—so what's the book?"

"The diary of an amateur lepidopterist," Doodle told her.

"Doodle is the person who found the title in our old card catalog," Carlos said.

"They just keep it for decoration," Doodle put in. "Nobody ever looks in it anymore."

"Nobody but Doodle," Carlos said. "But she brought me the card from the catalog, so I started digging around for it."

"We've found a few other rare titles that way."

Kai was beginning to see that Carlos felt the same way about books that Doodle felt about moths. It was the way that Kai used to feel about the violin. It was that thing that settled into a space inside you, and made you happy whenever you thought about it.

Or, at least, the violin used to do that for Kai. Thinking about the instrument now only filled Kai with loneliness.

"Can I take it home?" Doodle asked.

Carlos looked pained. "I can't," he said. "It's the only copy, Doodle."

"I know, but—"

"I'll keep it behind the counter for you. I won't let anyone else touch it."

Doodle hesitated, looking concerned. "Promise?"

"Of course!"

"Who else would want a book like that?" Kai asked, genuinely curious.

"Oh, my gosh!" Doodle yanked off the cotton gloves,

gaping over Carlos's shoulder. The librarian asked no questions—he simply pulled the book from the top of the counter and slid it onto the shelf underneath just as Kai turned to see Pettyfer approaching.

"Hello, *Miriam*," Pettyfer said to Doodle. "Here to do a little research?" He looked at Kai with his flat, blue eyes, and she gave a little shudder.

"I could've asked *you* that last night," Doodle snapped. "What were you doing by the graveyard?"

Pettyfer leaned ever so casually against the counter, unwittingly tempting Kai to give him a push and send him sprawling. She restrained herself. "I don't think I need an excuse to stand near my family's factory."

"Are you sure you weren't scouting moths?"

Pettyfer grinned with half of his mouth.

Kai resisted the temptation to smack the arrogant look off his face. She just wished he would go away. There was something about the smug coldness of him that made her furious and fearful, all at the same time.

Carlos's nose wrinkled, as if an unpleasant smell had just wafted his way. "I need to go . . . file something," he said, heading over to a book cart. He and Doodle exchanged a glance before he turned away.

Pettyfer's gaze drifted to the cart, then snapped back. "I might have been after a Sphinx moth," he said smoothly.

"Or you might have been hoping to steal whatever I got," Doodle replied, "after I got it."

"Why would I do that?" Pettyfer smirked his smirky smirk, sending a little shiver down the back of Kai's neck. "I've already got a project for the Lepidoptery Fair that's going to blow whatever sad little thing you're working on out of the water. A demonstration."

Kai couldn't resist temptation any longer. "Are you kidding?" She let out a loud snort.

The blonde lady slammed her book shut and glared at them. "Keep your voice down," she said in a loud whisper. "Some people are trying to study."

Nodding, Kai turned back to Pettyfer. "Are you kidding?" she repeated in a strangled whisper. "We are working on something so amazing that it'll probably make your brain explode and dribble out of your ears in clumps."

Doodle shook her head and looked at Kai with huge

eyes, silently telling her to cut it out.

Pettyfer looked doubtful. "Right. Like what?"

"Like it's a *surprise*," Kai snapped. "A *big* surprise! Like, the biggest surprise you'll see for the next hundred years!"

"Please. Miriam has tried to win that five-hundred-dollar prize for three years in a row. And three years in a row, she's lost. To *me*."

"Why do you keep calling her Miriam?"

"Because that's her name."

Kai looked at Doodle, who gave a little shrug. "Doodle is technically my *middle* name."

"And what's all this about five hundred dollars?" Kai demanded. She hadn't realized that the Lepidoptery Fair came with a cash prize. She looked at Doodle, who mashed her lips together and headed for the door.

"See you later," Pettyfer called.

"Not if we see you first," Kai shot back, adding, "Okay, okay, we're leaving," as the blonde lady let out a megashush capable of knocking the third little piggie's house down.

Doodle was already storming through the gate. Kai

hesitated a moment, unsure whether to follow. She had begun to think of Doodle as her friend . . . but was she, really? She hadn't said anything about the five-hundred-dollar prize, and Doodle wasn't even her real name.

Kai felt small, small as a dandelion seed. And as useless. She hated it—hated that feeling—but she wasn't sure what to do about it.

Doodle stopped. She turned. "You coming?" she asked Kai.

Kai remained on the other side of the gate. "When were you going to tell me about the five hundred bucks?"

"After we won," Doodle replied. "If we won."

"Why not before?"

"Because the Lepidoptery Fair is not about *money*," Doodle said slowly. "It's not about *winning*."

"What is it about?" Kai asked.

"It's about the *moths*."

That soft word, *moths*, hung there in the space between them. Kai felt her rage shifting, like the dandelion seed on the wind. It floated a moment, and then found a new direction—toward Pettyfer. "Okay, but we still can't let that . . . that jerk win."

"Exactly," Doodle agreed. "He doesn't care about the moths."

Kai thought. "Well, it *kind of* seems like he does. He's interested in them, at least."

"He's interested in *killing* them," Doodle snapped. "He pins them to a board while they're still *alive*, Kai." Doodle's voice was heavy with bitterness. "He isn't a lepidopterist, he's a *collector.*"

In Kai's mind, she saw a frail moth, wings flapping desperately as Pettyfer drove a pin through its body. She wished she hadn't imagined it. Now she couldn't stop imagining it, and it made her nauseated.

"He doesn't deserve to win," Doodle murmured. "He doesn't deserve anything."

Kai nodded. They couldn't let him win. They wouldn't. Because Pettyfer did deserve one thing—he deserved to lose.

The next day, the girls returned to the library. Carlos insisted that the journal was too delicate for the photocopier, but he let Doodle photograph the pages with her dad's iPad. Then they went back to Lavinia's house, and sat down at the worn gold-flecked Formica kitchen table. Doodle scrolled through the images as Kai poured out two glasses of a drink she had concocted over the weekend: Luna Juice, named for the bright green moths. It was a blend of lemonade and green Kool-Aid, and was surprisingly good. Plus, it turned your tongue green. Lavinia had quickly become addicted to it, and for the past several days there had been a pitcher at the ready in the refrigerator. "Hoo, girl, don't go giving out that secret recipe," Lavinia had said. "We're gonna make a mint! I've written ten poems since we started making this; I swear, it's good for the brain activity!"

"So, what are these, do you think?" Doodle asked now, pointing to an image of five lines, with numbers, on the screen.

"It looks almost like musical graph, with no notes. But I don't know what the numbers could mean."

"Look at this." Doodle enlarged another drawing. It was of an open-winged moth. The color was striking—pale blue, with white bands on the forewing and a large black-and-yellow dot that looked almost like an eye on each hindwing. "Irregular," Doodle said, pointing to the scalloped wing edges. "It's a Celestial."

Kai looked at the old peanut butter jar that Doodle had placed on the table. Inside were a stick, several fresh leaves, and the resin-coated blob that might or might not be a cocoon that might or might not be from a Celestial Moth.

"There's pages of them." Doodle scrolled through the images, showing a drawing of a moth at rest, one on a red flower, one in flight. After that were sketches of other moths, then some butterflies, then a bunch of praying mantises.

"*Someone* was really into bugs," Kai said.

"Everybody's got a thing," Doodle said. "What's yours?"

Reflexively, Kai said "violin" before she was even aware of the word.

"Really?" Doodle looked surprised.

Kai winced a little, half afraid that Doodle would ask her to go get her violin and play, and half hoping that she would. "Kinda."

"Cool." Doodle turned back to the cocoon. "It's just so hard to identify anything in this state."

Kai's fingers tapped against her thigh, playing out the familiar notes to her favorite Mozart piece. It was her thinking habit; she didn't even know she was doing it. "What should we do with it?"

Doodle sighed. "I don't know. Do you want it?"

"Don't you?"

"I'm not really sure how to figure out what it is. If it's a cocoon, the pupa is probably all dried up."

"Okay." Honestly, Kai did want the weird, fat little pearl. She liked the way it glowed in the darkness. She'd never seen anything like it.

"It's yours." Doodle pushed the jar toward her.

Several hours later, after dinner and a game (in which Lavinia took all of their Monopoly money, warning them to "Never talk money with a retired loan officer!"), Doodle went home and Kai took the jar up to her room. She placed it on the windowsill and then went to wash her face and brush her teeth. Kai changed into her pajamas, then shut off the light and sat on her bed, waiting for her eyes to adjust to the change. It took a moment to see the cocoon's soft glow. But then, there it was, shining dimly at the bottom of the peanut butter jar. It seemed friendly, somehow.

Could it really be the cocoon of a Celestial Moth? If so, the caterpillar inside must be dead.

Beyond the window, insects pulsed and hummed with a hundred different melodies. Kai didn't know much about insects, but she knew about music, and she could distinguish the cheerful creak of the cricket and the rhythmic buzz of the katydid. There were other melodies, too, and although she didn't know the players, Kai liked the way the sounds made her skin vibrate.

It was amazing to think that a cricket, a being smaller than her smallest finger, could make a noise that would travel across the yard, through her window, past her hair, and right into her ear.

There was another insect, one with a clear tenor. She loved the sound it made—every time she caught a piece of the melody, it reminded her of the cello.

Ah, there it goes again, she thought, straining to distinguish the sound from the many others.

It sounded so much like the opening of the second movement of Bach's Suite No. 1. *Did Bach like bugs?* Kai wondered, humming along. Filled with a sudden longing for her violin, Kai stood and walked quickly to the closet.

The black case lay in shadow, but Kai, knowing its familiar shape, kneeled and snapped it open. She reached for her bow, tightening and then rosining it carefully. She tuned up the strings, and then crossed to the window and sent a cool, clear note into the night. The insects seemed to pause for a moment as Kai played a melody that bubbled up from inside of her, and then the chorus swept over her and the hum and rattle from the grass and trees joined the notes like an orchestra.

A light blinked in through the open window and disappeared, like an ember winking out. Kai played on with her insect symphony, trying to cling to the notes, so that she wouldn't forget them. *I should write these down,* she thought. *The Bug Sonata.*

The lightning bug floated through the room, pulsing with occasional light until it finally came to rest on the bedside table. It glowed and dimmed and crawled across the pages of an open book.

The bug was crawling across the *The Exquisite Corpse*. The band played on as Kai dropped her bow and crept closer to peer at the page. There was a bit of new writing. The firefly lurched into the air and meandered out the open window. Slowly, Kai crossed the room and skimmed her eyes across the line.

Perhaps the music was a dream, it read.

THE EXQUISITE CORPSE

Perhaps the music was a dream.

Ralph blinked up at the whiteness overhead. A slender crack ran along the top of the wall, just beneath the place where it met the ceiling. He had just awoken, but he did not feel awake. He felt heavy, so heavy, as if he might sink through the mattress and into the floor. Through the floor, and into the ground.

His eyelids sank closed, shutting out the unfamiliar, white room. He did not wonder where he was. He did not care. He just wanted to sleep again, and perhaps to dream of music.

For a short while, there was no sound but the gentle rasp of his breath. Then a long, high note like a song.

His eyes drifted open. The music refused to be silent.

Light streamed in from a window near his bed. The

music pressed against the window, pushing against the glass like the soft pad of a cat's paw.

Ralph turned his head toward the light and sound.

A woman bustled in. Her dark hair was precisely parted beneath a round hat that perched atop her head like a stack of pancakes, and her long skirt swished at every neat little step. Her nose was fat as a cherry tomato and her cheeks soft and almost jowly. She smiled sweetly down at Ralph, and he thought how plain she was, and how kind she looked. "You're awake, then?" she said as she snapped the sheet back into place over him and tucked it up beneath his mattress.

"Where . . . ?"

"You're in the men's ward. Broken leg and a concussion—I heard you played a card trick on the wrong customer, tsk, tsk!"

Ralph winced as he tried to sit up. Another four years had passed, and Ralph was seventeen years old. He had become quite a cardsharp, and turned a tidy profit hustling other young men with a version of the shell game. But that career had its risks. He reached for the vial that he always kept in his pocket, and was shocked to find that he wore only a hospital gown. "Where's—?"

"All personal effects are stored in the side table."

Lunging for the table, Ralph let out a gasp, then fell backward onto his pillow. The nurse took pity on him and pulled open the drawer. "Is it in there?"

Ralph craned his neck, but was careful not to move his body. The drawer held a wallet. A watch on a silver chain. A set of keys. And a smoky purple vial with a silver top. "Yes," he breathed.

"Good." The drawer snapped shut, and the nurse reached for a dark metal crank at the end of the bed. With every turn, Ralph felt himself rise a fraction of an inch. "Your father's been by. Lovely man. Lucky you, to get this nice bed by the window. You'll feel better, looking out a bit."

Ralph placed a hand on his forehead. "Do you hear that?"

"Oh, Billy and his moaning? Don't mind that," the nurse said. "It's all in his mind," she whispered, pursing her lips and opening her eyes wide.

"No, I mean . . ." He turned toward the window, and the light fell across his face like a soft breeze. The wall was made up of three tall windows, each arched toward the ceiling in a curving hump. His bed was the closest to one of these, but the angle was such that he could only see the sky beyond, not the lawn.

"Oh! The violin? That's Miss Pickle." The nurse held out a small glass of clear liquid. "Drink this, you'll feel better."

Ralph wrinkled his nose. "What is it?" he asked.

The nurse cackled. "It's water! Honestly, did you think I was trying to poison you?" She laughed again, and held the water to his lips.

Ralph drank. He had never thought of water as having a flavor, but this was sweet and cooling. It seemed filling, too, like a piece of fruit. When he had finished, he leaned his head against the pillow. "Who is Miss Pickle?" he asked.

"Aren't you full of questions!" The nurse winked at him. "Well, I suppose you'll just have to get better and go see for yourself, won't you?"

The music curled through the men's ward, floating over the elderly gentleman in the large wheeled chair, and slipping past the man stretched on the bed beyond him. "How long will she be here?"

"Don't know." The nurse planted her hands on her hips and gave him a twinkly eyed frown. "She's a patient, too, but she seems quite well to me. I suppose you'll have to get better soon, or you might miss her."

CHAPTER EIGHT

Leila

THE SHUT AND SEALED windows couldn't keep out the smoky smell that hovered thick and insistent over the city of Lahore. "It's because it hasn't rained," Samir had explained. "Eventually, a monsoon will come and wash all of this away."

After their trip to the market, Leila's clothes held the city's smell. Her sheets even seemed to smell. She wondered if the smell had become caught on the inside of her nostrils—if even her nose smelled of smoke, and that was why she couldn't escape it.

She changed her clothes, but didn't feel fresher or smell better. Leila thought about Elizabeth Dear's signature fragrance—lilac body powder. *I need a signature fragrance,* Leila decided as she sniffed her smoky shirt. *Something to cover up whatever* this *is.*

Her computer pinged, and she walked (eighteen steps) to the bedside table to read the text. It was from her mother. "Good time to chat?"

"Sure," she typed.

Those four letters whooshed into space, bounced off a satellite, and then returned to Earth on the East Coast of the United States. A moment later, the computer rang and her mother's voice sounded through the speakers.

"Leila! How is it? We miss you!" her mom asked. As usual, she had the computer angled so that it showed a corner of her forehead and the curtain behind her.

"Mom, you've got to adjust it. Tilt the screen down—there you go. Over a bit. Can you see me okay?" Leila asked. Her parents were pretty terrible at video chatting, in spite of the fact that Leila's mother sat in front of a screen all day and her father was a computer expert.

The screen tilted, and her parents came into view. Her father's green-and-gray striped shirt stretched over his belly, and Leila knew he must have been sneaking into the chocolate halvah at night. "Hi, Daddy!"

He waved from behind his wife. "Hi, sweetheart!"

"Are you loving it?" her mom asked.

Leila thought about how best to answer. "Yes, loving it!" seemed like a lie. But "no" would set off alarm bells. "Everyone's nice." Leila glanced toward the window, looking out at the dome of the mosque. The smoke in the air made it look soft.

"How's the food? I'll bet they're stuffing you! Is the food good?"

"It's a little too spicy."

"I hope you aren't complaining!" Her mother's bright-red-framed glasses were perched on top of her head, and her hair looked like it hadn't been washed in three days. This was her Deadline Look.

"No, no. . . . It's great. Jamila Tai knows I love kabobs, so they're making extra ones for me."

"It's very generous that they're hosting you," her mother said.

"It's family!" Her father gave a dismissive little hand-flip away from his forehead, which Leila had recently realized was a very Pakistani thing to do.

"Yes, I know, it's nice of them," Leila said.

"You should buy them a gift while you're there."

"I gave them the stuff you sent along." Her mother had packed bags of chocolates and fancy soaps and perfume, which Leila had doled out the first night.

"That was nothing. This is really very gener—"

"It's family!" her father insisted. "I would hope that my own brother would be happy to have my daughter in his house!"

"Oh, Bilal." Leila's mother shook her head, and then turned back to Leila. "You wanted an international adventure like your sister's, and it's very nice of your aunt and uncle to give you this opportunity!"

This comment irritated Leila a bit. It felt like her mother was saying that Nadia found her adventure on her own, while Leila needed help. It might be *true*, but nobody wants to be *told* that. "It's great that you're getting to know Pakistani culture a little bit."

Leila's father huffed. "She knows Pakistani culture!"

Her mother held up a hand. "Bilal, please."

"Yeah—no, it's good. It's different when you're here," Leila said quickly. This was a familiar argument for her parents. Her mother often wished that Leila's father would teach her Urdu, or take her to the mosque sometimes. Her father insisted that he had never been religious when he lived in Pakistan, so he wasn't going to start now. As for Urdu, Leila and Nadia didn't even call their father Abu.

"So, uh—like what should I get these guys?"

"I don't know. Maybe something for the house?" Leila's mother was famously bad at choosing gifts, but she did have one good suggestion: "See what they like when you're out together, and just get that."

Her father rolled his eyes. "Then they'll get Leila something else! The gifts are nonstop! It never ends!"

"Bilal, I do not want Jamila to say that my child is so American that she didn't even know—"

"Okay, okay." Her father shook his head. "All right. You're right. I'm agreeing with you."

"Okay; I'm on it." Leila smiled and shook her head. It was comforting to think that her parents were at home, still being exactly themselves. "How are you guys?"

"We're great! Oh! I ran into Aimee's mother the other day. Aimee's been cast as Sleeping Beauty in the fall ballet—isn't that wonderful?"

"Yeah. Great." Leila didn't explain to her mother that Aimee wasn't really her friend anymore. She didn't mention the painful, gut-shredding conversation where Aimee had explained that she had more in common with Nadia, now that they were both in the same *accelerated* class. *Now Aimee and Nadia can be* remarkable *together,* Leila thought bitterly. She took a deep breath and filled the silence with, "Aimee has always been a great dancer."

"And have you been keeping up with Nadia's blog? She saw a lion!"

"Oh. Wow." Leila decided not to mention the parrot that she saw from the window. She couldn't think of anything to say that wouldn't seem pale in comparison to Nadia's amazing, spectacular cultural experience or Aimee's starring turn on the stage.

"I nearly had a heart attack when I read that," her mom went on, "but Nadia says it's perfectly safe."

"I'm sure it is."

"*You* should write a blog!" Her mom beamed. "Who cares if it isn't for school credit, Daddy and I would love to read it! Wouldn't we?"

"Of course," Leila's father said absently. His eyes had traveled to his lap, and she knew that he was checking his smartphone.

"The Wi-Fi's a little spotty. I'm not even sure it's possible." Leila didn't mention the secret blog that she was writing in her own mind. "Uh, listen, Mom—I need to go in a minute."

"Sure, honey. I love you! Don't forget to get the present. Just use some of the money we gave you."

"Thanks! I love you, too."

All of a sudden, Leila's mother burst into tears. "Oh, Mom," Leila said, touching the computer screen. "Dad! Do something!"

He looked up from his smartphone, and wrapped an arm around his wife. "We miss our girls," he said to Leila.

"I miss you, too."

"I'm sorry!" Her mother dabbed at her eyes. "I didn't expect to do that!" Another tear leaked out. Her mother boo-hooed some more, and her father said, "It's okay. It's okay, Sarah. Look—you have to cheer up! We can't go to the theater like this. We're supposed to be seeing a comedy!"

The theater? Her parents never went out. Leila knew it was unreasonable to expect her parents to sit around the house, doing nothing but working or missing their children. But she had kind of expected it, anyway.

"Good, good," her father said. "We'll speak again soon, all right?"

"Love you, honey! Love you!" her mother called. "Talk to you soon!"

I'll try to come up with some adventures for her before then, Leila thought as she smooched toward the screen, waving. "Okay! Bye!" Leila touched the keyboard with a finger and watched as her name disappeared.

With a deep breath (oh, let's be honest, it was a sigh), she sat down on the bed—on something hard. She knew what it was. For a few moments, she did not move, but simply continued sitting on the book. She began to count.

When Leila reached eighty-three, she realized that she was going to have to stop counting *sometime*. She would have to stand up *eventually*. The only alternative was to sit here, on this book, until she died.

Leila considered the pros and cons.

Ultimately, she lifted one leg and pulled out *The Exquisite Corpse*.

"What do you want?" she whispered. She turned the pages and stopped at the latest entry, which was about

Ralph waking up in a hospital, and hearing the violin. The name "Miss Pickle" tickled her ear.

I wonder if Ralph will meet her, she thought idly. Then, a moment later: *Well,* she reasoned, *can't I make them?*

The thought actually frightened her a little. But it thrilled her, too. *Why shouldn't I?* she wondered. She felt as if the book had been making all of the decisions so far. Leila would write a single sentence, and then the book would go off on a story of its own. And sometimes, more would appear for no reason at all, at least not a reason that she could figure out. It was a bit like her experience in Pakistan. She had said that she wanted to ride a camel, and go to the Shalimar Gardens, and visit Badshahi Mosque— but nobody seemed to be in a hurry to make those things happen. It was always, yes, yes, tomorrow, but when tomorrow arrived, it would turn out that there was some desperate urgent errand that could not be put off, unlike her sightseeing.

It was time to take some action. She couldn't let this book be in charge.

Leila pulled open the drawer in her bedside table and

selected a blue pen. *Ralph met Miss Pickle the very next day,* she wrote. She looked at the words for a few moments. After a while, they didn't seem to mean anything at all.

Finally, she snapped the book closed. Then she opened it again.

Nothing new had been added. Her sentence was still the last.

Thoughts swirled around her, thick as smoke, a strange mix of relief and disappointment, anger and surprise. Now, when she *wanted* the book to write something, it had nothing to say!

Maybe I stopped it, she thought. *When I tried to force it to do what I wanted, maybe I knocked the whole thing off course!*

She felt a bit proud of herself. *Hah,* she thought. *I finally shut you up.*

But, of course, she hadn't.

Everyone in the Awan family spoke English, but they did not speak it all the time. In fact, sometimes they would slip into Urdu without realizing they had. Once, her uncle even turned to her and said, "Isn't that right, Leila?" after everyone had been speaking in Urdu for almost twenty minutes.

"Right," Leila had said, but Samir caught her eye. He was laughing.

Leila didn't mind, though, when they lapsed into Urdu. It seemed more comfortable for them, and so it made her more comfortable. She liked sitting on the couch, surrounded by the Awan family as they chatted and argued and drank cup after cup of tea. Often, neighbors would come over, but after the first introductions, nobody paid much attention to Leila, which was fine with her. She had dreamed of coming to Pakistan and being a glamorous American, but instead, every time she was introduced, conversations seemed to center around how sad it was that Pakistanis sometimes lost their culture once they went to the States. Tonight, everyone was gathered in "the lounge," which was what Leila thought of as "the family room," to watch the latest installment of *Pakistan Idol*, which was both weirdly familiar and unfamiliar. The show's host spoke in Urdlish—an eighty-twenty Urdu-English blend—with a speech pattern that sounded like he had been taking lessons from Ryan Seacrest, which maybe he had. Rabeea had explained that the hosts were very famous Pakistani pop artists.

The show was down to seven contestants, and the night's theme was classic Bollywood songs. As Leila had gathered from her uncle's repeated explanations, "This is a classic. A classic from the 1982 movie . . ." Leila thought most of the songs were pretty awful, but she also hated all of her own parents' music, so maybe it was a generational thing.

Chirragh appeared in the doorway. He glanced at Wali, who slipped out of the room before anyone (with the exception of Leila) noticed. The small boy reappeared and crept over to Leila. "Someone has come here for you!" Wali whispered, wriggling with excitement.

"Not for me," Leila whispered back.

"Yes! It is!"

"How can there be someone for me?" Leila asked, but Wali was already shoving her toward the front door.

Chirragh stood at the entrance. He was smiling, which was how Leila knew that something horrible must have happened. When he saw Leila, Chirragh swung the door wider, revealing the goat boy.

The goat boy grinned when he saw her and said something in Punjabi.

Oh my gosh, Leila thought. *The goat boy is madly in love with me!*

This was a natural thought for someone who had read sixty-seven Dear Sisters novels. Of course he was madly in love with her! What else could it possibly be? Leila did not know how to proceed. How does one inform a goatherd that one is not interested in romance? Neither Elizabeth nor Jennifer Dear had ever encountered this problem.

The boy looked at her expectantly. In her mind, adoringly. He said something else, then looked at Wali.

"He wants the money," Wali translated.

"What?" Leila was confused. "What money?"

"For the goat," Wali explained.

That was when Leila registered that the goat boy had brought his white goat, which let out a loud bleat-squawk. Chirragh gestured toward the side of the house, as if he wanted the goat to go there.

"Why would I give him money for the goat?" Leila asked.

Wali began to look worried. "Because you bought

it," he explained. "You gave him five hundred rupees and promised the rest when he delivered the goat."

There was a long silence while Leila replayed the scene in her mind. She had given the boy five hundred rupees for a photo. Which was a rip-off. Wait a minute . . .

The goatherd said something sharp.

"He wants to know if the goat doesn't please you," Wali translated.

"No, it—it's a nice goat. Nice." Leila gave the thumbs-up sign, and then realized that this was the thumb that got her into all of the trouble in the first place. She yanked it back up her sleeve.

The goatherd's face clouded with anger, and he began to yell, which made Leila feel as if she were shrinking. Leila wished someone would close the door. She didn't want her uncle or aunt to hear this. She glanced at Chir-ragh, who looked disgusted. She turned to Wali, who seemed about to cry beneath the goatherd's shouts. "He's saying that you're tricking him—trying to get the price down!"

"How much does he want?" Leila asked.

Wali looked miserable. "Two thousand rupees.

Expensive—because of Eid."

That's two hundred dollars, Leila calculated. *Two hundred! Two hundred?* That was a ton of money, but she had it. She could just give the goatherd the money, and then he would stop yelling. But then, what would she do with the goat? Customs probably wouldn't let her bring it to the United States, and her parents would have a fit, anyway . . .

"I'm sorry, Leila! I thought you wanted a goat," Wali wailed.

"Why would I want a goat?" she asked. She wasn't being mean. She was honestly curious.

"I thought—I thought you meant it as an Eid present. For my family," Wali explained.

Oh. Oh! An Eid present? Right! He mentioned that Eid is coming up! Eid is a celebration at the end of the thirty days of Ramadan. But Ramadan is on a lunar calendar, and the date changes—it can fall at any time of the year. Leila hadn't noticed anyone fasting. Then again, the Awans weren't particularly religious. True, they had gone to Jumu'ah prayers last Friday, but did not seem to pray five times a day. So maybe they didn't fast, either. Leila's father certainly never did, and this was his brother's family.

So—the goat could be an Eid present. It wasn't a horrible idea. "But would your family want a goat?" She looked at the goat. It was about the size of a golden retriever. Maybe it *would* make a good pet.

"Of course!" Wali looked shocked at the idea that someone might not want a goat. "It's very traditional."

An image of her cat, Steve, as a kitten on Christmas morning popped into her mind. "Your parents won't be mad? Are you sure they want a goat?"

"They'd have to buy one themselves, if you don't get it."

"But they haven't picked one out?"

"Not yet."

Relief poured through her veins. This was brilliant. Brilliant! Her mom wanted her to get the Awan family a gift, the Awans wanted a goat, and *she had accidentally bought a goat*!

It was almost like fate. Leila thought about the fakir's blessing outside the ice-cream store. He said something about miracles—maybe this was one! *Thanks, magic fakir!* Leila thought. "Okay! Okay, I'll go get the money."

She hurried upstairs and pulled a stack of rupees from her suitcase. Then she handed it over to the goatherd, who was still sulking, under the impression that Leila had tried to swindle him at the last minute.

Please don't blame him. It had happened before.

Chirragh took the goat's rope and led it around the side of the house. The red henna flower on the goat's flank was the last thing to disappear behind the wall.

Leila placed a hand on Wali's shoulder. "Happy Eid," she said. "*Eid Mubarak.*"

"Thank you!" Wali said, scampering into the house.

A Good Deed Doer, Leila thought as she practically floated up the staircase, *that's what I am. A buyer of pets. Mother Christmas. This is going to make an awesome blog post!*

She had learned something new about her culture. Honestly, her mother was right about something: her father barely ever mentioned Pakistan, or his culture. He never told her anything. This incident made her feel terribly sophisticated. And it was all because of Wali and that stupid goat.

Leila felt so good that she didn't even bother checking

to see if anything new had been written in *The Exquisite Corpse*. She didn't think about the line she had added about Miss Pickle, or spend a single brain cell on the book at all.

But that doesn't mean that the book stopped thinking about her.

THE EXQUISITE CORPSE

Ralph met Miss Pickle the very next day.

Ralph's crutches chafed beneath his arms as he struggled to make his way out onto the lawn. The doctor had told him that he was lucky.

"A clean break near the top of the fibula, but not at the knee. You can put weight on it fairly soon." The doctor had a young face and hair that was rapidly disappearing. His pale blue eyes seemed genuinely happy to give Ralph this news. "I've put you in a gypsum dressing—the best thing for this sort of fracture—we can take it off in about four to six weeks."

Four to six weeks did not sound "soon" to Ralph. "Will I have to stay here for that long?"

"Oh, no. Your plaster should be set in another

twenty-four hours. After that, we'll have to keep you for observation. I'm concerned about the contusion you received on the head. You can probably go home in about ten days."

It had only been twenty hours since that conversation, but Ralph was tired of waiting. He backed himself against a rear door and pushed and struggled through the opening, barely managing to pull his fat plaster leg through before the heavy wood slammed shut. Outside, the sky slowly purpled as the sun sank behind jagged treetops bordering the wide green lawn. A bush rustled as a small brown rabbit loped, in no particular hurry, beneath the leaves as the sky above her changed as slowly as vapor rising from a lake. Sweet notes from a violin shimmered in the air like heat, pulling Ralph forward.

A girl with dark hair played her bow across the strings at the edge of the wood. Her eyes were closed as Ralph crutched his way toward her. When he reached her, he cleared his throat, so that she would know someone was close. She gave no sign that she heard until she was finished playing. Then her eyes—stormy ocean eyes—opened slowly, taking a moment to focus on his face.

"I know you," Ralph said.

"No, you don't," the girl replied.

"Yes—you're Melchisedec Jonas's daughter."

The girl turned her eyes to the dark woods. "He's not my father. He's my guardian." The word seemed to make her skin crawl. "I'm Edwina Pickle."

"I'm Ralph Flabbergast. Your guardian bought my parents' company."

"Yes . . . Flabbergast's Famous Kraut." She plucked a few strings. "I've heard all about what a horrible investment it was."

"You can't make that sauerkraut in a factory," Ralph said, his neck burning hot. "Small batches only."

"Don't worry. He's still rich. Besides, I don't mind seeing him furious."

Her eyes twinkled, like silver fish in a dark wave, and Ralph laughed as he studied her face. "We met once, remember? I showed you a magic trick."

"Yes . . . ," she said slowly. "Yes, I think I do remember."

"Why are you here? Are you sick?"

"It's my lungs," Edwina replied. "They've always been

weak. I've told Uncle Melchisedec that the air in the factory doesn't suit me, but he insists that I work there. The doctors are hopeful that fresh air will cure me."

Ralph did not know what to say. She did seem pale, but more from sadness than sickness. Her gaze returned to the woods, and Ralph saw something flutter there. It was pale blue and glowed like the moon. "Do you see that?"

"Celestial Moths," Edwina said. "They love the crepuscular light."

Ralph repeated the word: "Crepuscular?"

"The gloaming," Edwina explained. "The sunset. They also love the red flowers that grow at the edge of the woods." She smiled slowly at him. "Perhaps I can show you a magic trick," she said.

"There aren't many I don't know."

"Hm." She lifted the bow back to the strings and began to play a strange new tune. Her dark hair captured the warm light of the sunset as the moth made its crooked way toward them, hovering near the violin. It settled on the scroll, and seemed content to rest there. A smile curved at the corners of Edwina's lips as she played.

"You can make them come to you?" Ralph studied the

fat, furry insect. Antennae fanned, fernlike, at either side of its head, quivering above its vibrant blue body. On each wing was a spot, like an eye with a yellow iris, over a curlicue question mark.

"They like the music," Edwina replied. She stopped. The moth sat there for another moment, and then fluttered away.

"That really is magic." Ralph gazed at her in wonder. "Real magic, not the kind I do." He did not say that it was the kind he had been looking for his entire life, but he thought it.

Edwina seemed to understand completely. "Yes," she replied. "I know."

CHAPTER NINE

Kai

KAI STOOD IN FRONT of the closed door, unsure how to proceed. She had pressed the doorbell, but the way it dangled treacherously from a wire made her suspect that it wasn't working. She had knocked, but perhaps not loudly enough. And she didn't want to bang on the door, in case the doorbell *was* working and Doodle had heard the knocks, and maybe just hadn't had time to answer the door yet.

There are a great many details that go into planning even the smallest thing, as Kai's mother had taught her.

She had just decided to try knocking again, when she heard something—a rustling, scraping sound. It was coming from the side of the house.

Kai walked down the two concrete steps (one corner

had fallen from the top step and lay, like a shark's tooth, beneath the unevenly hung mailbox). Waist-high cornflowers, awkward on their leafy stems, clustered thickly against the edge of the house. Clumps of tall red-crowned bee balm punctuated a few clouds of black-eyed Susans. The grass was high and patchy, and the flowers seemed to have the run of the yard. They were wild, untamed things, planted without a plan. The result was colorful anarchy, a beautiful disaster.

When Kai rounded the corner, she found Doodle digging up a section of dirt beneath a bedroom window.

"What's up?" Kai asked.

Doodle looked up, her eyes taking a moment to focus on Kai, as if they had been looking down into the hole at the bottom of her shovel, seeing a new world down there. (They had.) "Hey. Just digging."

"What's that?" Kai nodded at a flower that lay on its side in an exhausted heap near Doodle's feet. The tiny flowers formed a purple cone, such a deep color that they looked like velvet.

"Butterfly bush," Doodle replied, waving at a tall shrub farther along the vinyl siding. "We've got a white one."

"That isn't white," Kai said. The bush was only partially white. More orange.

Doodle just lifted her eyebrows and walked over to the six-foot-tall bush. She gave it a shake, and the orange flowers lifted up, fluttering into a cloud and then dispersing. The bush was left with white blooms.

Kai cried out a single, incomprehensible syllable at the sight of all of those butterflies.

Doodle hushed her. "My dad's asleep in there," she said, motioning to the window.

"That's your dad's bedroom?" Kai asked.

"Yeah. He likes butterflies, too. I thought I'd plant this for him."

A harsh, rasping cough rattled the window, and Doodle froze. She watched the window with large eyes as the coughing went on for twenty-three seconds. Finally, it stopped. When it had been silent for more than a minute, her eyes lost their frightened look. "He's sick a lot," she said finally, not looking at Kai. "Sometimes, it gets really bad. Then he can't work. And when he can't work, he doesn't get paid."

"What does he do?" Kai asked.

Doodle nudged the dirt with the edge of her sneaker. "He makes coffins."

"Oh, right," Kai said, and Doodle looked at her sharply. "Lavinia mentioned it." Kai wanted to ask questions, but she sensed that Doodle didn't want to talk about it. *Maybe that's why Doodle holds back,* Kai thought, *because some things are too hard.* Kai decided to change the subject. "And is that little purple flower bush going to get as big as the white one?"

Doodle nodded. "They grow fast. So—what've you got?"

Kai looked down at the book in her hands. She had momentarily forgotten what had brought her across the street.

It was *The Exquisite Corpse*. She had tumbled out of bed and onto the floor, jolted out of a dream of music with the notes still lingering in the air. Her eyes snapped open to face the spine of the book. When she opened it, she read that Ralph had followed the music, too, and had met Miss Pickle. And then, there was another sentence. "There are those who long to know magic's secrets."

Somehow, Kai had felt that this was meant for her.

"Are you the kind of person who believes in . . . weird stuff?"

Doodle thought it over. "Like aliens?"

"No. More like magic."

Doodle sat down on the grass. Then she lay on her back, looking up at the sky. To Kai, it seemed as if a long time passed. The clouds twisted into new shapes, and Doodle stared up at them. At last, she sat up. "Everything is magic," she said. "The sky, the stars, the whole world. It's miraculous, when you think about it."

Kai shrugged. "Some things are more magic than others."

"Like what?"

Kai considered the question. "Well, like nursing shoes aren't magic. Checkbooks. Moths."

"Moths are extremely magical!" Doodle huffed.

"Okay, but, like, mud is not ma— Look, actually, I don't want to get into an argument about this." This was the thing that frustrated Kai about people. It was hard to know if they could ever understand you. Like the kids at school who thought she was "weird" just because she wasn't interested in hearing about who was currently crushing on whom. "I want to know if you believe in magic. Not the everyday kind of magic. I'm talking about, like, unusual magic. *Highly* unusual magic."

"I won't laugh," Doodle said then, unexpectedly.

Kai gaped. "W-what?"

"If you're worrying that I'll laugh at you about something, you can stop. I won't."

That was enough. Kai sat down on a patch of brown grass and handed the book to Doodle, who flipped through it.

"Isn't this your diary?" She cocked her head. "No—it isn't, is it? It looks old."

"Yeah—it's . . ." Kai took a deep breath. "I wrote in it, and it wrote me back. Now it's just gone off, writing its own story. I add to it, sometimes, and then it takes what I've written and makes it into a story. Sometimes, the handwriting even changes. Like—I don't know—like someone else is adding little pieces, too. And other times, it'll just go off and add more by itself, and I don't know why. Or how. It's, um . . . it's magic. A magic book."

"Wow." Doodle's gaze lingered on Kai's face, and then dipped back to the pages.

"Do you think I'm insane?"

Doodle looked up and held her gaze. "Not in this particular way."

"Do you think maybe I'm making it up?"

"Why would you make it up? I mean, I assume that you thought of all of the logical explanations, right? That someone is messing with you—"

"Right. Not possible. Sometimes, words appear if I close the book and just open it again. Almost instantly. So there isn't time for someone else to be writing in it."

"Whoa." Doodle held out the book. "Can you make it happen now?"

"It doesn't always work that way." But Kai leaned back to fish around in the pocket of her jean shorts. She came up with a ballpoint. Doodle handed her the book, but when Kai flipped it open, Doodle said, "No—don't."

Kai's hand hovered over the page. "Why not?"

"It's just—I believe you. Don't ruin it. Don't put something dumb in there."

"It'll just make it into part of the story."

"But if it's a *magic book*, Kai, you can't just—I mean, it's like drawing a mustache on the *Mona Lisa*."

Kai smoothed her hand over the golden lettering on the cover. She was overwhelmed with sadness, although she wasn't sure why. She had not yet learned that sometimes finding a true friend can make you feel even more acutely the loneliness of your life before that moment.

"The thing is, the newest part of the story was about a girl who played the violin. And a moth—it sounded like a Celestial Moth—came and landed on her bow. And I started thinking about those drawings in the lepidoptery journal . . . the ones that looked like music—"

"Maybe they are music." Doodle tugged a piece of grass and stared off into the distance, her mind miles away. "Moth music . . ."

"What should I do?" Kai asked.

Doodle looked up at the clouds. One of them had slowly formed into a shape that looked like a feathery wing. "Why don't you tell me the story?" Doodle suggested.

"The story in the book?"

"The whole story. What you wrote. What it wrote. Everything."

And so Kai did.

* * *

That evening, Doodle burst into Kai's bedroom with her usual uncoordinated cacophony. She carried the iPad in one arm, wiping the sweat from her forehead and into her hair with another. "Oh, man," she said, breathing hard, "I ran into Pettyfer on the way over here!"

"Blech," Kai said. "What was he doing?"

"He had something in a jar that he *said* was an Anna's Eighty-eight, which would be really rare around here, and he was all, 'I'ma Plastomount it!' and I was all, 'The hell you say!' but when I tried to grab it, he ran off and I chased him a while, but I couldn't catch up and I was afraid I'd drop my dad's iPad and I didn't want to miss sundown, so I came over here."

She flopped onto Kai's bed. "Man, it's hot today. That made me tired."

"All the running, or all the talking?" Kai asked drily.

Doodle just inhaled and exhaled for a few moments. "Can you believe he would kill something as rare as that?" she said to the ceiling.

Kai thought about how some people seemed to be missing something soft and human—something that allowed them to *feel things* for other people—and at that moment Melchisedec Jonas's name whispered in her mind.

"Yes," she said.

Doodle breathed a bit more, and then rolled onto her side. "That thing is looking lumpy," she said, eyeing the white cocoon/blob that sat in a jar at Kai's bedside.

Kai frowned. "It's been so hot. I think the resin is melting a bit."

Doodle sat up suddenly. "Are you ready?" She started scrolling through the images until she came to the page with the weird lines and numbers. "Here."

Kai looked at it. "I think it's a form of tablature. It's a really old way of writing music. Instead of writing the note, you write down a number to indicate the finger you're using, and the string. Guitar players still use a form of it." She had already pulled the black violin case from its temporary place in her closet. The black case was worn at the edges, and scratched. Kai had always handled it carefully; after all, it had been her father's. But anything that is used every single day for ten years will show wear. The silver clasps sprung open beneath her fingers, and she pulled the bow from its place. She tightened and ran rosin over the bow. Its weight was as familiar to her as her own arm as she tuned up the strings. Picking up her violin, she tested a few notes. The melody was eerily similar to the one she had been playing for the insects a few nights before. The one that had just . . . appeared on her fingertips. She was relieved that she still seemed to remember how to play. Before that night of the Insect Symphony, it had been four months without the violin.

"Every day, you make a choice," her mother always said. "To get better, or to get worse. What's it going to be?"

Every day, for almost ten years, Kai had chosen to get better, until the day—four months ago—she was told that no matter how much better she got, she wouldn't be the best. And if she couldn't be the best, the whole thing was a waste. She might as well quit.

Now, her fingers felt fat and stiff, like sausage stuffed into casing. She *had* gotten worse, but they still knew their places.

Beyond her window, the night chirped and hummed. She lifted the sash, letting in the song of the darkness.

"Do you think they'll come?" Doodle asked, her voice

hushed as if she were in a church. She sounded so hopeful that it made Kai's heart ache.

"We don't even know if they're out there. But maybe something will. . . ." Kai placed the violin beneath her chin and lifted the bow. She glanced once at Doodle—*four months since she'd had an audience.* She swallowed, then slowly drew the bow across the D string, pressing down her ring finger until she matched the note she heard outside. Then she hacked a quick series of chopping notes, over to the A . . .

Kai played according to the tabulature and the sounds it nestled in with the music of the night, at times joining the melody, at times adding a high harmony. She felt the notes lift from her violin, actually felt them rise, like something with weight, and join with the notes beyond the wall. She felt them braid together, becoming something heavy and large. Her eyes had no trouble reading the tablature—it was as if she knew the notes already, as if her muscles remembered them from long ago. She had almost forgotten that this was what it meant to play the violin: to become a part of something so deeply that you became almost invisible. She had disappeared, and there was only the music, the sound, the beauty, the reaching beyond yourself and becoming part of the fabric that knits everything together.

She played on and on until, finally, she became aware of a third strand on the braid of sound. A breeze lifted the white curtains until they fell back, like a sigh. Stopping, Kai turned to Doodle. "Did you hear that?"

"What?"

"It—it was like something was playing along. Matching my song." Kai played a few more notes, but nothing happened. "It's gone." She listened a moment longer. Nothing. She shook her head and swiped a finger across Doodle's tablet, to the next page of music. When her eye landed at the bottom of the page, she murmured, "Oh, my . . ."

Her voice evaporated—she had no breath to speak with.

Doodle looked at her sharply. "What is it?"

Glancing up at her friend, she touched the signature on the screen.

"What does that say?" Doodle craned her neck to see. "Edward?"

"Edwina," Kai told her. "Edwina Pickle."

Their eyes locked. Neither knew what to say, for they both realized at the same moment that there could be only one Edwina Pickle—the one who wrote a diary of moths and music must be the same as the one in the magical book.

"I'm scared," Kai said after a moment. "What does it mean?"

"I don't know."

"Should I—?" She glanced at the violin.

"I don't know," Doodle replied.

I won't play the rest, Kai thought. *I won't.* But—almost against her will—her violin nestled under her jaw and her bow traveled to the strings.

She played.

She played the sounds up to the stars, out into space, to heaven or wherever someone like Edwina might be, and she didn't stop until she heard Doodle gasp.

"What?" Kai cried. Her eyes snapped open; she had not even realized they were closed. "What is it?"

With trembling finger, Doodle pointed at the peanut butter jar on her side table.

"Oh, wow," Kai said as the cocoon—*jumped*.

Something inside it was alive.

THE EXQUISITE CORPSE

"Are you ready?" Ralph asked, holding up the folded piece of paper. He lay in his hospital bed, his leg raised, and Edwina sat perched on a chair beside him. She smiled, and Ralph let his eyes linger on the crinkles at the corners of her dark eyes.

"Do you want to read it out loud, or should I?" Edwina asked.

"You do it." Ralph handed her the paper.

Edwina unfolded it inch by inch, slowly revealing the alternating handwriting—hers, then his, then hers, then his again. Rain tapped and spattered against the tall windows, trapping them indoors. But Edwina had suggested a game of Exquisite Corpse, and so she and Ralph had passed a pleasant afternoon together, coming up with tale after tale. Each would write part of a story, and then fold it over so that only the last sentence showed. The other would then come up with the next part, and fold it again.

Edwina read aloud:

"Once upon a time there was a girl who lived in a hole. A horrible man had put her there, with no way to get out. It was a very deep and dark hole, and the girl was very lonely there.

"One day, the girl received a visitor. It was a mole. 'Hello!' said the mole. 'I am sure we will be good friends!'

"The mole lived underground, of course, but he didn't mind it. Sometimes, the mole tried to imagine what the sky was like. He had heard of it from an earthworm, but the worm's description didn't make much sense. Something about being quite the opposite of the hole: bright, and wide, but those words meant nothing to him, so he asked the girl.

"The girl puzzled over the words. Bright? Wide? What could they mean? She had lived underground so long that she had forgotten. One day, she decided to see if she could find a way out of her hole. She had to see the sky again.

"And so she asked the mole what to do. Naturally, the mole told her that she must dig!

"And so the girl did! She was a marvelous digger. As she went deeper and deeper underground, everything became darker and darker.

"'This must be bright,' she thought. 'This must be wide.' Then she saw something in the darkness—she pulled it out. It was a giant diamond. 'Ugh, worthless,' she said to herself. 'What use have I for a rock?' Just then, who should appear but her dear friend, the mole.

"'What are you doing?' he asked.

"'Digging toward the sky,' she said.

"'Have you found it yet?'

"'Yes, I believe so.'

"'Ah, how wonderful,' said the mole. 'I do love to be out in the bright, wide world.'

"And so they lived happily ever after, together, in the darkness underground."

Edwina smiled softly, and folded the paper carefully, crease by crease.

"I do love a happy ending," Ralph said.

"Yes." She looked up at him. "It's a wonderful story. Like a fugue, almost. Different strands that come together."

"Or like a magic trick."

"Yes."

"Yes."

Edwina looked out the window at the gray sky as

Ralph settled himself against his pillows. The heavy, weeping clouds made the long ward dim, but Ralph felt like the mole—happy in his darkness, uncaring of the wide world, and not at all lonely.

He was in love, and he knew it.

CHAPTER TEN

Leila

LEILA WAS IN THE yard in front of the Awans' house, thinking about what a lousy pet a goat seemed to make. True, the family had thanked her profusely and seemed really happy about it. But whenever Leila went out to the backyard to pet the silly thing, it would bang its head against her leg. It was pretty annoying. Leila had come out to the front to get away from her, leaving her tied up near a bunch of pretty red flowers that matched the design on her haunch.

The thick metal gate clanged open and a black car pulled into the driveway beside the small front lawn. The entire property was ringed by a high white wall, and topped with jagged broken glass. All of the large houses in the city were mostly hidden behind walls, with only their tops showing. It was one of the major disappointments of Leila's visit. At home, she loved walking around her neighborhood and looking at houses. Sometimes, she would even catch a glimpse of a room, or a family beyond the window. But here, nobody in her family seemed to go for walks anywhere, and there wasn't much to look at but walls, anyway. Each house in this area was its very own fortress.

The gate squealed closed and the black car was still for a moment before a back door opened and a tall man in a bowler hat stepped out. He stood, taking in Leila, who sat on a white wicker chair near a mango tree. She wasn't sure whether or not she should get up, so she was halfway out of the chair when Mamoo announced, "Samir told me about the book."

Leila fell out of the chair. It was a very inelegant fall— she tried to reverse her attempt to get up, then clutched at the armrest as her rear end missed the chair. Instead, she plopped onto her bottom and pulled the chair over onto its side next to her.

Mamoo made no move to help. It was impossible for Leila to tell whether he was surprised by her reaction.

Personally, I can tell you that Mamoo had lived long enough to know better than to be surprised by anything.

"I'm fine," Leila told him, scrambling to her feet and patting the dead grass and dirt from the back of her shirt.

"Yes, I see that." Mamoo helped her set the chair back upright. That was when she noticed that he was holding a thick, clothbound book in one hand.

"What's that?" Leila asked.

"The book," Mamoo replied, holding it up. He really did not think much of Leila's intelligence. "For you. Samir said that you were interested." The book was a dull red. *Kim* was stamped on the cover, and below that, *Rudyard Kipling*.

What is this? Leila wondered, at the same moment that she was flooded with relief that Mamoo had not been talking about *The Exquisite Corpse*. She had, in fact, left her air-conditioned room to escape from the book in the first place. Even when she placed it beneath her folded jeans and closed her bottom drawer, she felt that she could still hear it buzzing, like an insect. She knew it was there. She was always waiting for it to sneak up on her.

The night before, she had conducted another

experiment. She wrote the first sentence of her favorite Dear Sisters novel in the book. "Elizabeth Dear frowned at her reflection in the mirror, wondering who would mistake such a typical American girl—with her smooth cornsilk hair and sea-blue eyes—for a countess." Then she closed the book and waited. This morning, when she turned to the page where she had written the sentence, she found that it had disappeared.

The book had erased Elizabeth Dear! Leila suspected that *The Exquisite Corpse* was annoyed with her.

"Today we will go to see the gun." Mamoo pursed his lips, managing to point to the book in her hand with his silver mustache.

What? What? This sentence took a long time to worm its way through Leila's brain. Synapses went to work, connecting thoughts, until finally something lit up. "Kim's gun?" Leila said.

"Yes. And a trip to the Lahore Museum," Mamoo said. "Where is Samir?" He barked something in Urdu to his driver, who jogged into the house. A few moments later, he reappeared. Samir trailed behind. "Hello, Mamoo!" he called cheerfully. "Are you ready?" he asked Leila.

"Are we going now?" Leila asked.

"Yes, we decided last night, remember?" Samir asked. "Ami has to visit a cousin in the hospital and Rabeea is going with her, so today's a good day to see the gun." This plan *had* been discussed at length by the family the evening before. But, naturally, this discussion had taken place in Urdu. Leila had nodded and smiled whenever anyone looked over at her, and this was the result.

"Oh," Leila said. "Okay." She was happy to be going anywhere. She still hadn't even come close to getting her camel ride. When she suggested it, she was told her uncle was working, and her aunt was swept up in the daily tide of funerals and weddings and births and endless visits to sick cousins in the hospital that seemed to form the pattern of daily life in Lahore. The museum must have been settled on instead.

The driver hurried to open the doors to the car. Mamoo sat in front, and Leila and Samir sat in the backseat. Mamoo's driver was much more careful than Asif, but once they were off the quieter streets and onto the main thoroughfares, Leila still experienced the car trip as if she were inside a video game. Obstacles seemed to materialize in front of them at random and unexpected intervals—potholes, pedestrians, donkey carts, motorized rickshaws, once even a camel—and the driver's primary job was not to drive, but simply to avoid these things.

"There it is!" Samir announced, pointing to the middle of the road.

There, on a median, stood an enormous concrete block. Atop the block was a long, black cannon.

"Oh." This was not at all what Leila had pictured. She had thought Kim's gun was a revolver, or perhaps a shotgun. She certainly never expected to see it in the middle of the street.

"'Who hold Zam-Zammah, that "fire-breathing dragon", hold the Punjab, for the great green-bronze piece is always first of the conqueror's loot,'" Mamoo recited. Leila guessed that this was some quotation from the book in her hand.

"Would you like to get a closer look?" Samir asked as the driver guided the car to the curb.

Traffic darted past on either side of the median at the center of the street. "Not really," Leila told him. "I can see it from here."

"Nonsense," Mamoo announced, shoving open his door. The driver got out and stopped traffic. Horns beeped indignantly at him. Well, Leila didn't have much choice at that point.

"Sorry! Sorry!" she called at the honking cars and motorized rickshaws as she hurried after Samir to the center of the street. The moment she passed, they tore away down the street.

The median was long, and crowded with bowls of birdseed and large shallow clay pots of water. A throng of pigeons waddled back and forth, pecking casually. "What's all this about?" Leila asked.

"It's a *sadaqa*," Samir explained. "Feeding the birds is considered a . . ." He searched for the word. ". . . blessing? A good thing."

When they got closer to the cannon, Leila saw that it was on an island of sorts, and protected by a gate. "I guess they don't want anyone playing on it."

"That's how the book opens," Mamoo said thoughtfully. "Kim sitting on the cannon, refusing to give his friends a turn. All small boys are the same, I suppose."

Across the street, a beautiful brick building looked out

over old trees. At its four corners were minarets. "That's pretty," Leila said.

"That's the museum," Samir replied. "It's a landmark."

Leila turned again to the cannon. The wheels were massive and towered over her from their place on the pedestal. "It's made of iron and brass," Mamoo told her. "The people of the city gave their kitchen tools to make it."

"It seems so strange that there are flowers on it," Leila noted. There was writing, too.

Mamoo looked at her evenly. "Even flowers can be deadly."

"The writing is Persian," Samir put in. "The gun is called Zamzama, Taker of Strongholds."

"What's the book about?" Leila asked. "*Kim.* I haven't read it yet."

Mamoo's glance lingered on the cannon. "It's about a boy who goes on a search for a magical river with a Buddhist holy man."

"He becomes a British spy," Samir added.

Well, that spy part sounds good, at least, Leila thought. It sounded like the kind of thing that would happen to the Dears.

"Kipling's father was the curator of the Lahore Museum," Mamoo said. "Did you know that?"

Leila shook her head. "No."

Traffic sped past. Overhead, the telephone wires were lined with birds. Pigeons swarmed around their feet. The sky was full of smoke. And here was this massive cannon, this relic from another age, something from a story. Leila wished that she could think of something profound to say. The moment seemed to require something, but she did not know what to give it.

"I guess I've seen enough," she said at last.

Leila wasn't really a "museum girl," and the Lahore Museum didn't appeal to her at first. It had a bunch of stuff in glass cases. The usual things: weapons, jewelry, pottery. There were some rugs laid out on a platform. She was more interested in the uniformed guards, who carried scary-looking guns. They were mildly terrifying. Leila had noticed that there were guards everywhere in the city—even the ice-cream shop where she had taken Wali had a guard outside the door, now that she thought about it.

But Samir was interested in everything, and seemed to know a lot about the artifacts. He and Mamoo got into an animated argument over the possible uses of a Persian bowl.

They stopped before a radiant gold Buddha behind a red rope. Samir stood looking at it for a long time.

"My mom's kind of into Buddhism," Leila said. "I didn't know there were Buddhists in Pakistan." She was surprised by the collection of Buddha statues—a Buddha on a lotus, a Buddha in paradise, even a fasting Buddha that was all skin and bones.

"There were," Mamoo said. "There used to be everything in Pakistan. We are lucky these are still here. For now."

"What do you mean?" Leila asked. "Why wouldn't they be here?"

"Several years ago, the Taliban blew up the Buddhas of Bamiyan. I'm sure they would like to destroy these, as well."

"Those were Afghan Taliban, not Pakistani," Samir argued.

"They are all the same," Mamoo replied. "The Buddhas

were irreplaceable. I would have loved to see them."

They moved on. Leila felt a little differently about the armed guards now. She was glad they were there to protect the art. After another hour of trekking through the museum, Leila's brain felt tired. Samir wanted to take Leila to Lahore Fort, but Mamoo suggested that they return home for lunch. "We will see the fort another day."

"But Badshahi Mosque?" Samir said. "And the tomb of Muhammad Iqbal?"

"What do you say, Leila?" Mamoo asked.

"I really want to see the mosque. But . . . that sounds like a lot. And I'm kinda hungry."

"I understand," Samir said darkly. His arched eyebrow was higher than ever. Leila could tell that he was disappointed, and she felt guilty.

But she was starving. And half brain-dead from heat and museum artifacts.

When they pulled into the driveway of the Awan house, Asif ran toward the car waving his arms. Samir put down the window, and Asif looked at Leila, then spoke rapidly in Urdu.

"What is it?" Leila asked as Samir sprang from the car.

Mamoo leaned around the front seat. "Apparently, there is a sick goat."

"Oh, no!" Leila shoved open the car door, accidentally knocking into the kneecaps of Mamoo's driver, who had come to open it for her. "Sorry! I'm so sorry!"

The driver put up a hand in a manner that said both, "I'm fine," and "Please don't come any closer to me," so Leila hurried after Samir. She found him in the backyard, bent over the goat. The white beast lay on its side, shaking. It had been vomiting.

"What happened?" Leila wailed.

"You bought a sick goat," Samir snapped.

Leila felt betrayed by this accusation. "He was fine yesterday!"

Chirragh came through the back door with a bowl of milky water and a rag. Mamoo appeared and they exchanged a few words. Mamoo pointed to a bush with red flowers, and Chirragh nodded.

The goat gave a shuddering gasp and retched. Chirragh sat down beside her and dipped the rag into the milky water. Then he grabbed the goat's head and began to drip the liquid into its mouth.

"What's he doing?" Leila cried.

"It seems that the goat has eaten Scarlet Catsbane," Mamoo explained. "Chirragh knows a remedy."

Leila looked over at the red flowers. A blue-and-black butterfly was perched on a bloom, wings pulsing slowly, as if in meditation, or prayer. "Will it be okay?" Leila asked.

"My dear, I am a chemist, not a doctor. But Chirragh knows something of this sort of thing, and he believes the goat will recover," Mamoo said evenly. "As long as it is kept away from the flowers." Mamoo walked stiffly toward his car. His driver, who had been watching all of this from beneath a mango tree, dashed to the vehicle to open the door for him.

Guilt weighed down on Leila. After all, she was the one who had tied the goat near the flowers. True, the goat was annoying, but she didn't want it to *die*.

Samir petted the goat's fur, his hand smoothing over the red henna flower with the same steady beat of the butterfly's wings.

"What should we do?" Leila asked.

"Wait," Samir said. "I guess."

Leila thought about her book, and wondered whether

she should try going upstairs and writing a happy ending for the goat. But it had erased Elizabeth Dear. Would it take the goat seriously? *That book is the most useless piece of magic in the world,* Leila thought. *What kind of magic won't even help you save something?*

There really are some times in life when there is nothing one can do but wait. Later, when she was alone, Leila would write in her magic book. *Can't you cure her?* she scribbled, hoping that the book might somehow grant a wish. But she did not do that right away. She found that she couldn't leave the goat. She had come to think of it as hers, partly, and she felt responsible for its illness. So instead of going upstairs, she went to sit down beside Samir, and they both stroked the goat's fur until Jamila Tai called the children in for dinner.

THE EXQUISITE CORPSE

"Can't you cure her?" Ralph asked as he stood awkwardly at Edwina's bedside, leaning against his too-long crutches.

Edwina slept peacefully, her face resting in profile against the pillow. Her dark hair curled around her neck like a soft wave. Ralph longed to wrap a single curl around his finger, but he didn't dare. He didn't want to wake

Edwina or shock the doctor.

"She has been much improved of late," the doctor said. It was the same smooth-faced physician who had set Ralph's leg.

"Until yesterday," Ralph said.

"Until yesterday," the doctor agreed. "But we don't know what might have caused her to relapse."

The previous day, Ralph had waited for Edwina on the wide hospital lawn, but she had never arrived. Ralph crutched his way toward the rear entrance as dusk fell, and caught sight of a stiff, pale-haired figure dressed in black leaving from the side door. Ralph did not need to see the pale eyes to recognize the frigid air that followed Melchisedec Jonas.

Ralph shivered again at the memory. He knew that it was unreasonable, but he felt in his heart that a visit by Edwina's guardian had chilled her lungs.

"Rest is what she needs most," the doctor said. "Rest and fresh air. I've given her laudanum. She should have another dose in a few hours. The nurse will see to it. If Miss Pickle has a restful night, she should seem much recovered in the morning."

Ralph nodded good day to the doctor, then sat down

on a stool by the bed. He rested his crutches against the bed and gazed at her face. All he wanted was to stare at her face this way for the rest of his life.

Ralph started forward as Edwina gasped and reddened, her neck straining with coughs. The hacking lasted only a moment, and Edwina did not wake up, but panic had sunk its claws into Ralph's heart. What if she never woke up? What if she died?

If that happened, Ralph did not think that he could continue living.

He looked over at the bottle of laudanum by the bedside and his fingers traveled to his pocket where the silver vial lay. Once the thought had entered his mind, he could not get it to release its grip.

Ralph looked around. The women's floor was quiet. An unfamiliar nurse made a bed at the far end of the room. Patients were sleeping or out for air and exercise.

With the quick fingers of a cardsharp, Ralph removed the vial from his pocket. Carefully, he unscrewed the cap on the laudanum bottle and placed it on the table. Then he tapped a few smoky grains of magic into the medicine.

"Make her well," he whispered.

Then he closed both bottles. It was the third and final wish, but it was the only one that had ever mattered.

Edwina turned her head, murmuring something in her sleep. Ralph leaned forward, and thought he caught the whispered words, "dear old mole."

Ralph believed in magic, and although fear and love held him in sharp talons, he allowed himself to fly away on the feathered wings of hope.

CHAPTER ELEVEN

Kai

KAI SHIFTED IN HER pew while her great-aunt listened to the violin, eyes closed, her round body tipped backward like a globe tilting on its axis. Kai had been to church plenty of times—she and her mother went nearly every weekend—but she had never been filled with the desire to strangle someone in a holy place before, and it was making her uncomfortable. It didn't seem very church-y.

Pettyfer was up at the front, playing the violin—the *violin*!—and it was all Kai could do to keep from screaming. For one thing, the piece he played was simple, something any advanced beginner could master, but he wore a smug, superior, unfaltering smile even when he made a mistake. For another thing, the violin was exquisite. Kai knew violins, and she knew it had to cost at least ten thousand dollars. And Pettyfer wasn't that good.

Kai loved her violin. It was only worth a fraction of Pettyfer's, but it had been her father's. And Kai had *earned* that violin. Her mother had promised her that she could have it when she "was good enough," and that moment didn't arrive until fourteen months ago. It had taken years of playing two hours a day to earn it.

And Pettyfer—

Gah!

She wanted to grab the violin and smash it over his head—except not *that* violin, it was too nice. She would go buy another, cheap violin and smash him with it.

Kai looked up at the stained-glass window picturing Jesus with a lamb on one side and a lion on the other. *Doodle is a much better person than I am,* she realized. *She would never want to smash a moth on Pettyfer's head.*

When he finished and took his smug bow, Aunt Lavinia opened one eye and looked at Kai from the corner of it. "He sure is a *special* boy, now, ain't he?" she murmured. A thousand sparks of meaning glittered in that crystalline sentence, like the sun drying up the raging storm in Kai's heart. The minister stood at the lectern and announced a hymn. The organ hooted and hymnbooks thumped and rustled as people struggled to find their place, and a moment later, Kai tumbled into the music and let herself sing. Her chest loosened with every note.

After the service, Lavinia had to greet just about everyone in the small church, introducing her "darling niece, Walter's girl." Kai had to say "thank you," as people told her how much her father had meant to them. They would grasp her hands, look deeply into her eyes—one old blue-haired lady even burst into tears. Kai gave her an awkward pat, half wishing that she could burst into tears, too. But her father died when she was three, and she barely remembered him. She couldn't just cry on demand.

"Was my father very religious?" Kai asked, once the woman had dried her tears on her sleeve.

"Oh, not terribly," Lavinia told her in a low voice. "Church is just something we did on Sundays."

"Why didn't anyone mention his music?" Kai asked.

"Oh, Walter didn't play in public much until he was older."

Kai nodded. She knew that it had been her father's dream that she would have the opportunities for violin that he'd had—and that she would surpass them. Her mother told her so whenever she hit a snag in her practice, or had trouble mastering a new piece. *Well,* Kai thought, *that's over now.*

Once they had greeted everyone in the church, including the minister, they made their way out the wide double door and started toward the parking lot. A giant white Lincoln Navigator stopped short in the middle of making a left-hand turn onto the road. A white-haired gentleman in a wheelchair was rolling through the crosswalk, and the Lincoln had stopped to avoid hitting him. Unperturbed, the man carried on crossing the street toward the church as the driver blasted a loud, long honk.

"Mmm-hmmm." Lavinia pursed her lips and strode right up to the SUV, where she knocked on the tinted window, which rolled down at a smooth, unhurried speed.

The man who looked out had blond hair and a flat, gray expression. His paunch nearly touched the steering wheel, and the air-conditioning blasting from the vents ruffled his hair. The woman beside him had tresses that were a highly unlikely shade of blonde and ten fingers stacked with diamonds. She looked straight ahead through the windshield while her husband glared at Lavina. "What?" he demanded.

"Brother Pettyfer, I was just wondering if we could count on your support for the Places for People project," Lavinia said smoothly, leaning an elbow on the car window as the white-haired man rolled up onto the sidewalk and passed by, glowering at the car. "You know, the youth group is going to be building houses for some of last month's flood victims."

Pettyfer Senior huffed. "Why don't those people get flood insurance? Or move someplace that don't get flooded? Why do they got to live so close to the swamp?"

"The land is cheap by the swamp," Lavinia told him.

"Come on, Dad!" someone whined from the backseat. "Let's go!" Kai wrinkled her nose at Pettyfer's nasal whimper. He ignored Kai, and she was happy to return the favor.

"Everyone in this town wants money," Pettyfer Senior snapped. "Don't I pay enough in taxes?"

"I'm sure I have no idea," Lavinia replied sweetly. "Do you?"

Kai giggled and the blonde woman finally looked over

in her direction. "Let's go, Petty," she said.

Pettyfer Senior stared hard at Kai's great-aunt. "Sister Lavinia, nobody will ever learn to stand on their own two feet if people just give them money."

"Oh, I see. And what about people who inherit their money? How do they learn to stand on their own two feet?" Lavinia asked, but the dark window was making its smooth way back up. The Lincoln's tires screeched as it made the left turn.

Lavinia planted her hands on her hips, then looked up at the sky. "Forgive me, Jesus!" she shouted.

"What? Why?" Kai asked. "You didn't do anything wrong. You just asked him to help with a project."

"Hmm." Lavinia lifted the eyebrow over her big eye. Her gray hair was twisted up and fastened with a beautiful carved comb. In her hot pink tunic and white slacks, she looked elegant and more than a little intimidating, and Kai was—frankly—slightly surprised that Pettyfer Senior had barely given her the time of day. "Oh, there isn't any Places for People project, I just asked him that so that he'd have to turn me down right in front of the church," Aunt Lavinia replied. Her smile was half embarrassed, half proud of her mischief. "I told a lie on a Sunday! Oh, I'm so bad!"

"Well . . ." Kai wasn't sure what to say. It *was* kind of bad. But it was better than smashing a violin over someone's head.

"Sometimes, I think I should learn to be more kind." Lavinia glanced up at the church tower. "But then I think—forget it; I'm too old to worry about being nice to someone like that Pettyfer."

Kai reached out to touch her aunt's elbow. "Me, too," she said.

Doodle, as usual, didn't knock.

The next afternoon, Doodle didn't even slow down when she saw that Kai was playing the violin, she just strode right into Kai's room and plopped herself onto the unmade bed saying, "Don't mind me."

Kai didn't—she just kept right on playing through the piece, which was one of her favorites, Beethoven's Violin Sonata No. 4. The final note ran through the room, skimming the walls and shimmering at the window. Kai opened her eyes.

"Wow," Doodle said. "You're . . ."

"Rusty."

"I was going to say incredible."

Kai huff-snorted, as if the compliment had been an insult. "I'm *rusty*. Did you hear how I was sharp there, near the end? It sounded *awful*." Kai tucked the violin into its case and, with three quick twists, loosed the bowstring.

"I thought it was amazing," Doodle replied. She peered over at the peanut butter jar. "How's the patient?"

"Nothing new to report."

Doodle cocked her head. "How long have you been playing?"

"About an hour. I really should do two, but I don't—"

"No, I meant *in your life*."

"Oh. Since I was three." Her thumbnail picked at the calluses at the tips of her fingers. They had softened in the months she had stopped playing, but now the strings were wearing familiar grooves in the tough fingertips. "I haven't practiced much lately."

"Really?" Doodle grabbed a rumpled pillow and shoved it behind her back, so that she was half upright. "Why not?"

"What's the point?"

"What do you mean? Isn't music the point?"

"I mean, what's the point of practicing? I'm never going to be a concert violinist, so. . ." Kai slid her bow into the sleeve. Then she placed the violin into the velvet-lined case and snapped it closed. The windows were shut, and the room was hot and still. It was too hot to open a window, and too hot to leave it closed.

"How do you know?" Doodle asked.

Kai sat cross-legged on the wood floor. It was cooler there than anywhere else, but the wood quickly absorbed the heat of her body. "I know because I know. Because I don't have what it takes, okay?"

"Really? What does it take?"

Kai thought it over. "More."

"Well, you could still just play. For fun."

"I don't think it would be fun without . . ." Kai searched for the words. ". . . without the dream."

"What dream?"

"The dream to be—" Kai shrugged. "My dad always dreamed of being a concert violinist."

"Oh, so, wait. Was this your dream? Or was it your dad's dream?"

"It was—mine," Kai said. "Both." But Kai knew that this wasn't quite true. Her dream wasn't to be a concert violinist. Not exactly. It was more like, her dream was to fulfill her dad's wish. To make it come true. Because he wasn't around to do it himself. Because it seemed like the thing that had to be.

"Anyway, I blew it," she said. "I ruined everything."

"How?" Doodle asked.

Kai sighed. She looked up at the ceiling. How could she explain? It was about having a father that was dead, and a mother who worked too hard for years to make up the difference, and then lost her job, anyway. It was about how, no matter what you did, sometimes things didn't work out. She closed her eyes and said, "I didn't get into Susan Laviere's studio."

"Who's Susan Laviere?"

"She's a violin teacher. She's the best in the country. My dad—my dad wanted to study with her."

Kai looked over and Doodle nodded, not like she understood, but like Kai should keep going.

"My dad loved the violin, and when he was in high school, he got into Susan Laviere's studio. But his father, my grandfather, wouldn't let him go. He wanted my dad to be a doctor."

"Did your dad give up the violin?"

"No—he was a professional musician. He played weddings, art receptions, and stuff like that, but he really wanted to be a true concert violinist. He always thought he could have been, if he had studied with Susan Laviere. That's what my mom says. He wanted me to have the chance that he missed out on."

"Isn't she still teaching, though?"

"Yes. She's old, and she only takes three new students a year. Usually, she only takes people who are in high school. But my violin teacher submitted a tape, and I auditioned." Kai spoke up to the ceiling. It was easier to talk without looking at Doodle.

"And you didn't get in?"

"No. We found out the same week my mom lost her job. It was a disaster."

"Your mom got fired?"

"No way." Kai shook her head. There was no way her mother would ever get *fired*. She had been the top regional salesperson for the past three years, and even got to drive a shiny silver Lexus as a reward. "Her company was reorganized, and her job didn't exist anymore. They offered her something new, but it was less money and a lot of travel, and she's a single mom, so—"

"So forget it."

"Right. And now I'm here while she looks for work and takes a three-week course on computer skills—social media, all that stuff. It just stank because it was like we both failed majorly in the same week after working like crazy for . . ." Kai shrugged. "I don't know. Maybe after that, it was better to be apart for a while."

"But you just said Susan Laviere usually only takes people in high school."

"She took a middle school kid this year." Kai reached for the fringes of the rug that lay beside her bed. She let the silk strands dangle over her fingers, then let it go. "It just wasn't me."

"But you can try again next year. You'll be better by then."

"So will everyone else."

"Are you . . . you're really just *giving up*?" Doodle couldn't believe it. She was honestly trying; she just couldn't quite manage it.

"I'm telling you, I heard those other players. They're better than I am."

"So—you're not going to play? At all?"

"Every time I play, I think about my dad, and how I let him down."

The other thing Kai thought of each time she opened her violin case was her mother's face as she read the rejection letter, and her expression when she turned to Kai.

"So—is that what you were thinking of, just now?" Doodle asked. "Your dad?"

"Well . . . I was. The first couple of times. But then, something happened."

"What?"

Kai nodded at the peanut butter jar.

Doodle bolted upright. "Has it moved again?"

It had twitched the first night, and then lay still, no matter what Kai or Doodle did.

"It moves every once in a while," Kai explained. "I think it depends on what I play."

"Does it like the music?"

"Yes, but it's particular. It only likes when I play the . . . uh . . . buggy music. Watch." With a shrug, Kai opened her violin case, tightened her bow, picked up her violin, and nestled it into position. She paused, nodding at the jar with the cocoon, which still sat on her bedside table. Then she began to play the night music, the sounds of the crickets and rain on the leaves, the rattle and hum of the insects and worms as they burrowed into the earth.

Kai stopped and both girls stared at the cocoon. Once more, the white bundle jumped and dangled.

"It did it," Doodle whispered.

"It doesn't always happen." Kai played a few more notes. The cocoon was still, and then jumped.

"Holy grasshoppers," Doodle said. "You have to do a demonstration at the Lepidoptery Fair!"

"You think so?"

"Kai, I swear, this cocoon is like—who knows how old. Maybe as old as Edwina Pickle! And your music is *waking it up*!"

Cold fear washed over Kai. "Maybe it's a coincidence."

"Maybe it isn't! Maybe these cocoons need a certain

kind of music—a certain frequency—to open!" Doodle jumped up and danced around the room, jigging madly.

"It may not even *be* a cocoon . . ."

"Don't you see it?" Doodle pointed. There was a tiny tear in the long white lumpy pearl, a scar running from end to end. It was opening. "Don't you *see*?!"

Kai's fingers felt thick and heavy. What did it mean—that the cocoon was hatching (molting? Kai wasn't sure of the word) after being frozen in resin all of this time? It frightened her.

"Play!" Doodle urged. "Play! Don't stop now!"

Kai forced her fingers to move, slowly at first, then more quickly as Doodle kept on dancing. The cocoon was quiet now, perhaps resting after its efforts, or perhaps frightened into stillness by Doodle's frantic dance. But Kai played on and—for the first time in four months—saw something other than her mother's disappointed face just beyond the violin strings.

At dinner that night, Aunt Lavinia wore a strange expression. "I heard you playing that violin tune. Where did you learn it?"

"I . . ." Kai wondered how much she should say. "I read it in an old book."

"Yes; I think it's quite old. I've heard it before . . . long ago. . . ." Lavinia's eyes were far away. "Somewhere."

"Have you ever heard of someone named Edwina Pickle? We think she wrote the music." Kai's words came out all in a rush.

Lavinia shook her head. "Pickle? No, sugar. I think I'd remember that name."

"What about Ralph Flabbergast?" Kai asked.

"Ralph Flabbergast?" Lavinia repeated. "Why, yes, I've heard of *him*."

Kai gasped. "Did he live around here?"

Lavinia had taken her hair down from its twist, and the silver waves hung loose around her face. Her eyes met Kai's. For the first time, Kai realized that her aunt's irises were a very similar color to her own. An unusual light brown ringed by black. It was strange to see her own gaze reflected back by someone else. It was disorienting and comforting at the same time. "He lived *exactly* here," Lavinia replied at last. "He was my dear old uncle."

THE EXQUISITE CORPSE

Ralph crutched his way out to the wide lawn, beneath a sky soft with clouds. Despite the awkwardness of his movements, he managed to hobble quickly. The notes fluttered and floated, shimmering like soap bubbles, as he shouted, "Edwina!"

"Mole!" she shouted, as she removed the bow from her violin and then ran—ran!—toward him. She looked as if she wanted to throw her arms around him, but instead she reached for his hand and gave it an affectionate squeeze.

"I'm well! I'm quite well!" Edwina twirled, and her serge skirts swirled about her ankles.

"I can see that," Ralph said. Her cheeks were pink, and her eyes sparkled. Her joy made her almost radiant.

"She gave the doctor quite a shock." A young man with an earnest expression stood up from a wicker chair and walked over to join them. He held out a hand. "I'm Edwina's brother."

"Parker," Ralph said. "Good to see you. I don't suppose you remember me, but we met long ago."

"I do remember." Parker's eyes crinkled at the edges.

"And even if I didn't, Edwina has told me so much about you that I feel we're friends." Parker's words were kind, but his face was troubled, and Ralph felt his joy evaporate a bit, like steam in cold air.

Edwina plucked a few notes on her violin. "The doctor says I may be able to go home as soon as next week," she told Ralph.

"Yes," Parker said. "But Edwina, we mustn't be hasty."

"Dear brother, we'll see how hasty you are to leave a hospital once you've spent six weeks there."

"I do hope the company hasn't been too dreary," Ralph said.

Edwina smiled. "On the contrary, dear old mole, the company is all there is to recommend the place." She narrowed her eyes as a figure in white strode purposely toward them. "Oh, bother. Here comes Lucille. I'm sure the doctor wants to listen to my lungs again with that dreadful cold stethoscope. I've been avoiding him all morning. Can't he see I'm well?"

"Please do as the doctor says, won't you?" Parker asked, putting a gentle hand on his sister's arm.

She looked appealingly at Ralph. "Don't look at me,"

Ralph told her. "You'll never escape Lucille. She's like a dog after a rabbit, and the rabbit is you."

Lucille truly did look like a bulldog, and—with a sigh—Edwina called, "All right, all right. You've found me at last! I surrender," and trooped toward the nurse.

Ralph and Parker watched her go for a moment. "Her recovery is truly a miracle, isn't it?" Parker asked.

Ralph nodded, unable to contain his joy. "It's magical."

"Yes . . . that's the word that Edwina used." Parker cocked his head, and placed his hat at a jaunty angle. "Mr. Flabbergast, you are my sister's friend. May I trust you with a—private matter?"

"Of course."

Parker gazed off toward the woods. "Mr. Flabbergast, you are aware that our guardian is a man with a certain reputation."

Ralph hesitated. He didn't want to say anything unkind about Edwina's guardian. "I have always heard it said that he was a good man of business."

Parker looked at him plainly. "I will say that he is not a kind man. In fact, I have met spiders that are kinder."

"And less bloodthirsty," Ralph agreed before he could stop himself.

But Parker just nodded. "Good. So we understand each other. While it grieved me that my sister was ill, I always felt there was a certain . . . security here. At the hospital."

"Security—from your guardian?"

"In short, my sister and I are heirs to a large fortune. I believe, though I cannot prove, that our guardian has been poisoning her."

Ralph gasped as bile burned through his stomach, churning up muck and acid. "Poisoning her?"

"I know it sounds impossible—but he makes her work at the casket factory, and the place clearly makes her ill. And then, the very same day that he comes to visit her here, she falls ill again?"

"But why aren't you ill?"

"I don't know! I can't explain it! But my sister has always been sensitive. And you've met my guardian—his very presence is poison!"

"Can't you explain to Mr. Jonas that the factory makes her unwell?"

"He knows. I'm convinced that is why he continues."

"Yes . . ." Ralph frowned. "But you don't seem to fear him." His voice held the unspoken question: Why?

"I fear him. But not for my own sake. Our parents died

when I was quite young, and they never altered their will to include me. The will states very clearly that Edwina is the heir, and, after her, Melchisedec Jonas."

"But surely you have a claim?"

Parker's smile was wretched. "Melchisedec knows that no one is likely to challenge him in court. Not any of the courts around here—he has paid off the judges. And I certainly won't dare if something happens to my sister. Ralph . . . I don't want her to return to our house."

"But what will she do?"

"I have been offered a teaching position. A prestigious one, teaching at a new mission school. There's a place for Edwina, as well, teaching small children, if she will come. Now that she's well, we have the opportunity to get away. The voyage might even do her good, but it can do her no more harm than being forced to work in the factory or live with our guardian."

"Voyage? Where?"

"To India. The Punjab. Mr. Flabbergast, you will convince her to come, won't you? As her friend, you must. I beg of you."

India? Ralph wanted to say. But India is full of dangers! She cannot leave me!

He looked up at the evenly pale gray sky, like an ocean of mist. He felt lost in it as his mind spun, trying to find a new answer. How could he keep Edwina here? What option did he have? He could not ask her to marry him—he was barely seventeen, he had no money, and her guardian would never allow it.

"It's for her sake," Parker said.

A single raindrop, cold as a pinprick, fell against Ralph's arm, as he thought of the vial in his pocket. The cruel vial that granted wishes—wishes that were granted, but with a disappointing end. A tree hit by lightning. Delicious sauerkraut that almost made them rich. Ralph looked into Parker's eyes, eyes that were so like Edwina's, and yet so different, and although he opened his mouth to say no, no she could not go, not even to save her, no, the word that came out was, "Yes."

CHAPTER TWELVE

Leila

LEILA DID NOT LIKE this turn of events. *The Exquisite Corpse* had now followed her to the bathroom—or perhaps gotten there first—and was propped up on a towel bar, waiting for her, when she turned to wash her hands.

"Have you ever heard of *privacy*?" Leila asked. She took the book out to her room and walked the twenty-three steps to the bed. There was no point in trying to put the book away. It wanted her attention, clearly, like a puppy with a Frisbee in its mouth. With a resigned sigh, she flipped through the handwritten pages to the latest section and ran her eyes over the entry.

When she reached the part about Parker and Edwina leaving for India, she stood up. Then she sat back down again, until she read the word *Punjab*, and then she stood up again.

Lahore is in the Punjab, she realized. *And Pakistan would have still been part of India when Edwina was alive.* Fifteen steps to the bureau, and Leila grabbed a pen from the jar she kept there.

Are you trying to tell me something? She scribbled in the book. She closed the book. She counted to fifty. Then she opened it again and let out a little scream.

A new sentence had appeared.

I thought you were trying to tell me something, it read.

Kai

ALL THE WAY ON the other side of the world, Kai sat on her bed. The heavy evening air, ripe with rain and mosquito-thick, had driven her inside. She was reading the newest entry in the book when a scribbled message began to appear: *Are you trying to tell me something?*

Her heart's regular rhythm sputtered and faltered. *What?* Her mind bucked and spun, like gears unable to catch. *What?*

Fingers trembling, she pulled a ballpoint from her jeans. Her breath was shallow and quick; she couldn't get enough air.

I thought you were trying to tell me *something,* she wrote.

Letter by letter, the reply appeared. *I don't get your story. What does it mean?*

Kai sat back, taking in this message.

She had found the story about Ralph and Edwina confusing. She had found the magic book mysterious and a little frightening. She had found the link between Ralph Flabbergast and her aunt Lavinia to be—unlikely to the point of bizarre.

But this was even weirder. She had always more or less assumed that the book knew what it was doing. That it had a point, as books do. That it was telling a story. And yet, it seemed as if the book were now trying to make her captain of the ship.

You're writing it, she pointed out to the book.

But you started it.

Kai had to admit that this was true. *Barely! It isn't my story,* Kai wrote. *It's yours.*

I'm not making it up!

Kai stared at the words. She had the feeling that she wasn't understanding them properly, as if they were coming through on a lousy radio.

Well, I can tell you that she wasn't. She didn't know that she was writing to Leila. She didn't know Leila existed.

And Leila didn't know about her.

The book knew, but wisely kept silent.

Are you saying it's real, then? Kai wrote.

You tell me.

Ralph Flabbergast *was* real—she knew that much. He was Lavinia's uncle. Edwina was real. She and Doodle had read her journal—and seen her signature there on the pages.

Yes, it's real, she wrote.

She waited for the reply. Finally, it came.

I want a happy ending, then.

Don't we all, Kai thought, her fingers hovering over the page. *Well, make it happen.*

How?

Kai didn't know how to reply. She set the book down on the bed.

Hello?

Hello?

After a moment, the words began to disappear. Letter by letter, from last to first, the words sparkled silver, then seemed to sink into the page until everything that had been written that evening was gone.

Kai didn't know what to think of a book that was confused about its own story; that wanted her to tell it its ending.

Of course, the book knew the ending. But it was a very intelligent book, and knew that the best stories only give enough information to keep the reader interested. It wasn't about to start explaining too much. Instead, it let Kai wonder.

I don't know the ending, Kai thought. *How can I?*

But if I don't and the book doesn't, either . . .

I guess nobody does.

THE EXQUISITE CORPSE

"This came for you today," Mrs. Flabbergast said as she handed Ralph a parcel wrapped in brown paper. "Feels like books."

"Yes, books," Ralph said.

"Don't you have a library card?" she demanded, but Ralph was already headed upstairs. His leg had healed, but for the rest of his life, he carried a slight limp that was especially pronounced on cold, damp days.

In the month that he had been released from the hospital, he had visited Edwina in her home five times. Each time he saw her, she seemed paler and thinner. Blue veins were visible in her forehead and at her throat. She seemed tired. But she was not ill. Although the cold company of Melchisedec Jonas seemed to exhaust her, Ralph's wish kept her reasonably well.

Tonight, Ralph would see her for the last time. Tomorrow morning, she was set to take a train to the port, where she and Parker would board a steamer for New York City. They would sail to England, and from there, around the Cape of Good Hope, up the Eastern Coast of Africa, and finally to Karachi, where they would begin their overland journey to Lahore.

"I expect it will take us two months to get there," she had told Ralph the last time they were together. "But, oh— think of it! India!"

Ralph had wanted to ask her if she was sure it was quite

safe. His mind reeled with thoughts of snakes and tigers and terrifying unknowns, but he remembered his promise to Parker. "And is the school open yet?"

"Oh, yes. Apparently, the Britishers have been opening schools and churches. There are plans for a very grand one called Aitchison out beyond the edge of the city—it's supposed to be the grandest school in Asia!" When Edwina spoke of her journey, she recaptured a bit of her glow. And so Ralph told himself that it would be all right. That, although the journey was not exactly safe, it was safer than life with Melchisedec Jonas.

And so Ralph acted eager and excited whenever he was with Edwina, and saved his worries and tears for when he was alone.

Now, in his room, Ralph slowly unwrapped the package. Inside were two leather-bound volumes. The Exquisite Corpse. Ralph had seen the book advertised in the newspaper, and so had ordered one for himself and one for Edwina as keepsakes.

They had arrived from Kalamazoo, Michigan, just in time for Edwina's departure.

The books were lovely, printed with gold and inscribed

with instructions for playing the game. Let the magic begin! *it read.*

Magic is forcing us apart, *he thought.* If I had never wished for a cure . . .

He was wistful only a moment, until another voice spoke up. Well, what then? She might have died instead of merely going to India! As it is, she can return in five years, when she fully inherits the factory. And in those five years, you can work, and save, and wait.

What's five years to someone in love? An eternity, of course. But an eternity that's worth waiting for.

Ralph turned to the first blank page of each book. He would write their names in each one. He dipped his pen in the inkwell, and his eye landed once again on the word magic. *He traced his fingers over the letters.*

Magic, *he thought, and sadness—fine and pale as mist— gathered in his heart.*

Putting aside the pen, Ralph pulled the vial from his pocket. He knew that there was no magic left inside, but he still couldn't help wishing. He filled the vial with ink, screwed on the cap, and shook it, hoping for some sort of alchemy. Then he poured the ink back into the well.

I wish that, one day, we might continue our parlor game, *Ralph thought as he dipped the steel nib of his pen and began to write the names.* I hope our stories will fill the pages of these books—forever.

CHAPTER THIRTEEN

Leila

A BLACK KITE WHEELED in the dust-gray sky. Leila watched the bird glide lazily, only bothering to flap its enormous wings when it was absolutely necessary to keep itself aloft. It didn't seem to be hunting, or doing anything in particular besides enjoying the feel of the air and the sun and the view from far above.

It wasn't lonely.

Not like Leila.

When Nadia brought up the idea of going to Kenya, she had told their parents that spending the summer in a foreign country would be "fun" and an "educational opportunity." But, so far, Leila's own adventure had only taught her that she was much smaller than she had ever realized, and the world was much larger—and stranger.

Leila missed the afternoons she used to spend with Aimee, just leafing through magazines, gossiping about celebrities, discussing Dear Sisters books, munching Doritos, trying new hairstyles, watching movies. But those days were over, anyway. *Ta'Mara is your best friend now*, Leila scolded herself. It was true, in a way—Ta'Mara was the best friend Leila had. But Ta'Mara wasn't really Leila's Best Friend, and Leila knew it. Ta'Mara was nice, and she was funny, but she and Leila didn't always connect. Being with Ta'Mara was a bit like being in Lahore—unfamiliar enough to be slightly uncomfortable.

Here, nothing was easy. Leila didn't feel like she could just turn on the television without asking for permission, or even instructions, and even if she could, none of her favorite shows were on. She couldn't make her own snack without bothering the servants. She couldn't go anywhere without a strange magic book trailing after her, trying to get her to figure out what it was supposed to be about.

The sun beat down, making the air feel thin. It was hard to breathe. Still, air-conditioning gave Leila a headache, and the generators ensured that the Awans never had to endure the blazing heat. Babar Taya had insisted that this was the coolest summer in the past ten years, but it was over 110 degrees, and so Leila scuttled between the too-cold indoors and the too-hot outside in an unending loop.

Still, Flower always seemed happy to see her. The silly goat would prance around at the end of her lead whenever Leila came into the yard. She had recovered quickly from her bout of Red Flower Disease, and was now back to her proud, prancey self. Leila patted her absently until she wandered off to stand on the edge of a rock. There were walls around the garden, and so Leila found herself looking at the sky.

A door creaked behind her, and Rabeea stepped out, pulling it closed behind her. "Where are you sneaking off to?" Leila asked.

Rabeea jumped at the sound of her voice. "What? Nowhere! I'm not sneaking! I didn't know you were out here." She tucked her handbag under an arm and adjusted her peacock blue duputa. The straps of a cloth bag dangled from her wrist. The sun wasn't brilliant, but Rabeea's black hair was styled straight and gleamed across her stiff shoulders. "My mother knows I'm going out."

"I was just kidding," Leila replied. She felt her neck burning beneath the sun. Somehow, she always managed to say the wrong thing to Rabeea. It was more than just a language barrier; it was that Rabeea always assumed the worst possible interpretation for Leila's words.

"Oh," Rabeea said. Then she turned and headed toward the car, motioning for the driver. She gave him the bag without glancing in his direction.

"Where are you going?" Leila asked, and Rabeea turned back to her.

Her eyes were guarded. "Shopping," Rabeea replied.

"Hm."

Rabeea sighed. "Do you want to come along?"

The goat butted at her leg. Leila shrugged. "Sure."

Rabeea wished that she hadn't asked, and it showed, which sent a secret flash of joy through Leila. Besides, Leila didn't have anything to do except look at the sky and get all wrung out by the heat, and there was only so much of that she could take. Asif held the door for Rabeea, and Leila went around to the other side of the car and yanked open her own door. Asif smiled at her as he passed the window. She got the feeling that he found her amusing. She didn't mind.

He rocketed through the gate and down the street. Several turns later, they maneuvered into traffic, where they had the usual death-defying experience of attempting to get through the congested streets of Lahore. Rabeea gave directions in machine gun Urdu, and Asif replied "Gee, hanh," to everything as he steered around some obstacles and created others. Rabeea didn't speak a word to Leila, which was fine with her.

Finally, they pulled into the parking lot of a giant concrete building. It was the usual combination of shops and offices, and didn't look like it could have anything to offer a hardcore shopper like Rabeea. She took the cloth bag from Asif, and Leila followed her cousin toward a jewelry store. She was surprised when Rabeea passed it by, heading for a staircase beside the shop. Two men holding lit cigarettes watched as the girls climbed a flight of concrete stairs. Then they climbed another, and Leila followed Rabeea into an ugly and industrial gray hallway with windows that were simply empty squares cut from concrete. A pile of rough lumber was piled at one side, and many of the doors had numbers that were falling off.

"Where are we going?" Leila finally asked in a jagged gasp. She wasn't exactly sure where they were, and the place seemed deserted. She had the sudden fear that they were about to do something terrible.

Rabeea ignored her, and came to a stop in front of a wooden door bearing the number 333 below a pale blue circular window. Rabeea pushed open the door, and Leila stepped into a room with brilliant white walls hung with works of art—three large calligraphic paintings hung beside a portrait of two women in vibrant saris. At the center of the room was a golden sword on a pedestal, a brilliant blue butterfly perched at the tip of its blade. A pretty dark-eyed girl about Rabeea's age kneeled on the floor, wrapping a brown paper parcel. She was chatting with someone—a certain handsome, mischievous-haired boy—as he casually leaned against the wall, texting on his phone. He looked up when they walked in and gave them a smile.

"Took you long enough to get here," Zain said. "Hey, Leila." His eyes skimmed from her face to her shoes, then back up again, and Leila felt her heart fall to the floor, like she'd just shot upward on a fast elevator.

"*Helaam,*" Leila muddled in a blend of Urdu and English, giggling nervously.

"It's not my fault we're late," Rabeea snapped, clearly implying that it was Leila's fault, which was not true.

The girl wrapping the present smiled up at Rabeea, who bent down to give her a kiss on the cheek. They chatted excitedly in Urdu, and the girl gestured at a wall hung with sculptures made of nails welded together to look like faces.

"Shireen, do you know Leila?" Zain asked, yawning like a lazy cat.

"No." There was an elegance in Shireen's voice that Leila admired, and her dark eyes sparkled. "As-salaam alaikum." Shireen smiled shyly.

"Wa-alaikum asalaam," Leila replied.

"Shireen, this is my cousin," Rabeea said. "Shireen's mother owns the gallery."

"I didn't know there were art galleries in Lahore."

Rabeea looked at Leila as if she were a complete dolt. "Of *course* there are. Don't you know anything about Pakistani artists? Sadequain? Shahzia Sikander?"

"South Asia has a rich history," Shireen said generously,

clearly trying to ease Leila's embarrassment. "And the art community is wonderful. Full of talent."

"If you think a bunch of nails welded together and stuck on the wall is art," Zain put in.

"Zain never likes the contemporary exhibitions," Rabeea said. "He likes the old stuff."

"What do you think of all this?" Zain waved his hand to include the entire gallery.

"I don't know anything about art." Leila crossed to a wall to inspect a quartet of portraits. They were images of animals. "I like these."

"One day, we'll have some of Rabeea's art on these walls," Shireen said, smiling at her friend.

Rabeea held up the cloth bag. "I brought you the brushes."

"You're into art?" Leila asked. "Seriously?"

"Rabeea is very talented!" Shireen laughed. "Didn't she tell you? She has been helping my mother with the classes she teaches at the orphanage. You're always so generous," Shireen said to Rabeea as she accepted the bag of art supplies.

Leila remembered the moment in the car, when Rabeea

had told her not to give money to the poor. Leila had thought that she had a heart of granite. It had not occurred to her that the fact that Rabeea did not help *everyone* did not mean that Rabeea never helped *anyone*.

"I'm so glad those girls can paint with your mother. It means so much to them." The sadness in Rabeea's voice touched Leila, and surprised her. She wondered what else Rabeea thought about, what else she might be hiding. Those questions embarrassed Leila, for the very fact that she never thought to ask them before.

Rabeea's eyes drifted to the portrait of two old women, their arms full of bangles. They were laughing. She gazed at the image as if it had taken her somewhere, as if she saw things in it beyond simply what was there, something so beautiful that it actually changed her face, softening it. Rabeea's glance made Leila want to experience the same thing. She looked more closely at the pictures on the wall before her. They were portraits of animals, each decorated with flowers and henna, and the artist had painted them so that you could really tell the personality of each. A camel gave a smug sideways smile, a bull stared aggressively at the viewer, a lamb looked sweet and innocent, and the last one—a goat with red flowers in its forelock—had eyes that spoke of mischief. Shireen came and stood beside her. She was tall and graceful, and reminded Leila of a willow tree.

"Do you like it?" Shireen asked.

"That one looks like Flower," Leila said. "My goat."

"You have a goat?" Rabeea asked, coming over to join them.

"Well—*your* goat. The goat I bought. I call her Flower because she has a henna flower on her leg. I got her for Eid," she explained to Shireen. "She got sick, but she's better now."

"What was wrong with her?" Shireen asked.

"It ate something," Rabeea explained. "A plant. Chirragh says it will be no problem for Eid."

"Chirragh makes the most delicious goat." Zain smiled, waggling his eyebrows.

"Oh, this goat isn't for eating," Leila said quickly. "She's for Eid."

Zain laughed as Rabeea and Shireen exchanged a glance.

"She's a *gift*," Leila explained. "A pet."

"Oh," Shireen said, turning wide eyes to Rabeea.

"Don't be stupid," Rabeea snapped at Leila.

Zain pursed his lips, but Leila could tell that he was suppressing a smile. Her stomach clenched cold, like fingers over ice.

Flower is a pet, she thought. *Right?*

Right?

Rabeea stared at her a moment, as if she was about to say something more. Then she seemed to think better of it, and took a deep breath. She turned to the sword at the center of the room. "This is incredible," she said as she walked away.

"It's hand-forged," Shireen told her, trailing after her friend.

Zain's mouth twisted into a smirk that made Leila shudder, so she looked away from him, back at the animal portraits. Then she turned to an image of a sky full of colorful kites. A placard explained about Basant, a kite festival that inspired the image.

Zain watched Rabeea inspect each piece. The way he smiled at Rabeea told Leila everything she needed to know about why he was at the gallery in the first place.

Leila was not the star of a Dear Sisters romance. Rabeea might be, but she wasn't. So much for *that* adventure.

Once they had looked at the art, Zain took everyone out for sweets and tea. Leila wasn't hungry. Leila didn't ask Rabeea anything else about the goat, not even on the drive home. She couldn't bear it.

And so they were silent, each lost in her own thoughts.

That night, Leila found Samir in the library. He was lying on the couch, propped up with a mountain of pillows snatched from every chair in the room. "Hello," he said cheerfully, putting aside his book.

"Where is everyone?" Leila asked.

"Downstairs," he replied. "They're announcing the top ten on *Pakistan Idol*."

"You're not watching?"

"I only watch the shows where they sing." Samir settled back against the pillows. "I detest the elimination shows."

Leila looked around the room, and considered asking a few questions about the desk, the books, anything. But that wasn't why she had come looking for Samir. There was no point in putting it off any longer, and even though she suspected that she knew the answer, she had to force herself to ask the words. "What is Eid al-Adha?"

Samir's smile faded under the devastation in her face. "It's a holiday. When Abraham offered to sacrifice Ismail to God," he said gently. When Leila didn't reply, he went on, "It was a test of faith. Allah commanded Abraham to sacrifice his son. When Abraham told Ismail this, he agreed to be sacrified. But when Allah saw that they were faithful, the sacrifice became a ram." Samir watched her face carefully. "You've never celebrated it? You've never even heard of it?"

"I thought Eid was when you gave money, and wore new clothes and stuff." Beyond the window, for once, the smoke had lifted. Usually, it collected the light from the city, making the night sky almost gray, but tonight it was black as tar.

Samir sat up. "That's the other Eid. That comes at the end of Ramadan, Eid-al-Fitr."

She felt those words like a cut from a sharp knife: it took a moment to feel the pain. "The other Eid," she repeated.

"Yes. In this one, you sacrifice an animal, and give one third to the poor. One third you keep yourself, and a third you give away to friends and family." Samir closed the book he had been reading and laid it on the table beside the couch. He came and stood beside her. "You didn't know? Why did you think we wanted a goat?"

Leila couldn't tell him. She couldn't get herself to utter the word *pet*; it sounded too ridiculous to her now.

"Where are you going?" Samir called as she raced through the door. "Hey!"

The image of Zain's smirk stabbed at her as she flew down the stairs. Dimly, she heard Samir's voice, and even felt his footsteps following her, but she didn't look back. She blasted through the fancy kitchen and even Chirragh stepped aside as she tore through the real kitchen and out the rear screen door.

Flower was her goat. *Her* goat.

Her goat darted away as Leila barreled into the yard. "Come here," Leila said coaxingly. She took a step toward Flower, who leaped backward with a loud bleat. "Come back!" Leila cried. "I'm trying to save you!"

"What are you doing?" Samir asked as the goat raced around the lawn with Leila chasing it, shouting, "Come back! Come back!"

"Catch it!" she cried. "Stop it!"

"Why?"

Flower leaped and dodged until finally Leila got the idea to corner it. She grabbed a table as Flower neared a corner of the wall. She shoved the table against one wall, and placed her body in the gap.

"Don't do that!" Samir warned as Leila leaped forward, shouting, "Got you!"

But the goat leaped onto the table, and, from there, to the top of the wall.

Leila would have been amazed at the jump if she weren't so horrified. "Get down!" she cried, just as the goat leaped down to the other side of the wall. Leila stood facing the wall, as if some part of her expected the goat to leap over again, back into the yard. After a few moments, she turned to face Samir.

He was baffled. "What were you doing?"

"I just—I just wanted to help Flower." Leila looked up at the top of the wall. "It doesn't matter. I'm glad she's gone. She's free."

"Until someone finds her and takes her home," Samir said. "Then she will be *their* dinner."

Leila sat down, right there, on the dark grass. She had not thought of that. Again. The world around her blurred as tears blinded her. *I'm such an idiot,* she thought. *Nadia never would have let this happen. Ever. No wonder Rabeea thinks I'm stupid. No wonder my parents expect so little of me. And Flower—poor Flower!*

Samir sat down beside her. They were silent for a moment as Leila's tears fell, and fell, and finally cleared. She swiped at her cheeks.

"I have to go after her," Leila said at last.

Samir looked at her closely. Leila waited for the cutting remark, the insult that never came.

Instead, Samir said, "I'll come, too."

It was dark, but the neighborhood was not quiet. In fact, it was just beginning to come alive as visitors made their way between houses. Still, Leila wasn't used to being out in the city at night, especially not one that seemed to be unaware of the invention of the sidewalk. A sleek Toyota Camry rolled past, and the driver honked at them. Chirragh shook his fist.

"Is this a good idea?" Leila whispered to Samir as the

servant limped after them, slowing them down. Samir's father had insisted that the servant come with them, and had made them promise not to journey farther than the nearby mosque.

Samir turned his cocked eyebrow on her. "Is it a good idea to be out after dark looking for a goat?"

Leila wiped a damp palm on the pink cotton of her shirt. "Well, I was actually talking about . . ." She glanced over her shoulder, where Chirragh limped and glared. She looked back at Samir and whispered, "*him.*"

Samir stopped short. "Are you joking?" His face was a solid fence of surprise.

"No, I—" Leila sneaked a furtive glance at Chirragh, who had halted at a respectful distance. "Don't you think he's *scary*?"

Samir stared at her, clearly flabbergasted. "Chirragh has worked for our family his whole life! He's the most trustworthy man in Lahore, and he is very loyal to our family."

"How can you be so sure?"

"When he was young, Chirragh was a house servant. He was injured in a bus accident, so he couldn't climb the stairs very well. Many people would have dismissed him, but my grandfather insisted there was a place for him, and then my grandmother taught him how to cook." Samir's eyes met hers. "That's why he's the best cook in the city."

"What would have happened . . . if your grandparents hadn't let him be the cook?"

Samir's right shoulder rose, then dipped. "There are a lot of poor people in this city. And some of them are desperate. I can't even imagine their lives. . . ." Unconsciously, he looked over at Chirragh. "Sometimes, when servants can't work, they have to beg. If they get sick, there are no doctors, or they can't afford them. Some families treat their servants horribly, because they know they won't dare to leave. But Dada Jaan, our grandfather—he always said that everyone under his roof was his responsibility. Abu and Ami say the same."

Leila looked over at Chirragh, who was still waiting and glaring. He lifted his chin sharply, as if to signal that he knew that they were talking about him. As if he were daring them to judge him.

Leila felt guilty for having been so suspicious, and for assuming he was a villain. That guilt blended to homesickness, and she wished she could drop right through the earth to the other side, to her small, messy, pale purple room. Where things were simple and adventures never happened.

In the silent moment that followed, an insect with dimly glowing wings jolted awkwardly between them, and flew on.

Leila watched it begin to disappear up the street.

They didn't have to speak. Both she and Samir followed the moth.

The moth seemed to want to lead them somewhere, as every now and again it would circle back to them and then flutter lurchingly away. They didn't really know where they were going, so when it turned a corner, they followed. Once they were halfway up the side street, they saw it disappear over a wall.

"How odd," Samir said, seemingly to himself.

A moment later, they heard a strange sound, half moo, half bleat.

"Flower!" Leila stared at the wall. There were places here and there where bricks stuck out in an artful pattern—it was perfect for a climbing goat. "How can we get in? Should we try to climb over?"

Samir pressed a bell at the gate. "This is Mamoo's house," he explained.

A small metal peephole was pulled back, and a pair of dark eyes appeared. The height of the window suggested that the speaker was not very tall. Samir and the man on the other side of the gate exchanged words in Urdu, and finally the window was closed again. "This way," Samir said, motioning to a metal door at the side of the gate.

Leila followed Samir through the door and was courteously greeted by a small, stoop-shouldered man in a cap and a long gray beard. Chirragh was the last through, and he greeted the man as if they were acquainted. The servant spoke cheerfully and unceasingly to both Samir and Leila, who nodded as if she understood. The small courtyard in front of the house was elegantly bricked and fragrant with flowers.

Samir spoke a few more words, and the man clapped, then trotted away. Samir trotted after him, and Leila—unsure what was happening or what to do—hurried after them both. Soon, she found herself in a small rear yard, where a goat was bleating, protesting the rope that had been looped around its neck. There were three large urns set on the ground, spilling over with red flowers, which glowed softly with the light of moths. At first, Leila thought that the insects were humming, but after a moment, she realized that the music poured from a nearby window. A fourth urn lay on its side; dirt and red flowers littered the ground. A lone moth sat on one of the scattered flowers. The man pointed to the urn and spoke rapidly, then shook his finger at Flower, who pranced in the corner.

"He says that the goat knocked it over," Samir explained.

Leila looked at the red flowers. It was the same kind that had made Flower sick before. "She's not a very smart goat, is she?"

"Smart enough to get away from us," Samir pointed out.

After moving the flowerpots a safe distance away, the servant led them into a simple front hallway and through a wooden door. Chirragh remained in the hallway as Leila and Samir tiptoed into the living room. Mamoo was seated in a large gold velvet chair, his eyes half closed as he listened to music that floated on the hiss of a proud-looking, dusty old contraption in the corner. The moth sat at the edge of the wood, perfectly content. Leila and Samir waited until the recording ended and his eyes snapped open.

He looked at them for a long moment, as if he couldn't quite place who they were. Then, suddenly, he said, "What brings you here at this time of night?"

"You've got our goat," Samir told him.

Mamoo pursed his lips. "That goat is guilty of destruction of property."

"He's already under a death sentence," Samir pointed out.

"It's a her!" Leila wailed. "And we've got to save her!"

"What's this?" Mamoo cocked an eyebrow, and for a moment, he looked a lot like Samir.

"I bought the goat," Leila confessed. "I didn't know it was supposed to be dinner! It was all just a big, stupid—" Her voice caught, and she couldn't finish.

"She feels responsible," Samir said. He did not actually roll his eyes, but Leila felt she could hear something like it in his voice.

"It's *my* goat."

"Are you a vegetarian?" Mamoo asked politely.

Leila blushed. "No."

"Hm," Mamoo said.

"That's different. I'm not responsible for those animals—the ones I eat. I'm not a vegetarian, but I don't go around killing people's pets and eating them." She looked at Samir and his mocking eyebrow. "You don't get it, do you?"

"I understand it," he said. It was gentle, an apology.

She turned to Mamoo. "Do you get it?"

"Is it important for me to?" His voice was not cruel.

"Yes! Well . . ." She thought it over. "No," Leila decided. "Not as long as you help me, anyway."

Mamoo nodded, as if he approved of this answer, and crossed over to the contraption. The moth fluttered for a moment as he wound the crank and placed the needle on the record. The violin began again with its strange, uneven melody and peculiar chirps, and the moth settled back down.

"What is that?" Leila asked.

Mamoo smiled dreamily. "Do you like it?"

"I'm not sure," Leila admitted, and Samir kicked her.

"Yes," she corrected herself quickly.

"It's not to everyone's taste," Mamoo said. "This is a recording of my dear auntie."

"Who?" Samir looked puzzled.

"Edwina Auntie," Mamoo said. Samir still looked puzzled, so he went on, "She was the sister of my father's employer and dear friend. One very interesting thing about Edwina Auntie is that she came to Lahore with her own coffin."

"She was *dead*?"

"No," Mamoo said. "She simply brought a coffin with her. My father told me that Edwina's guardian was such a miser that he gave it to her instead of a steamer trunk. He was in the coffin trade. Her brother brought a Dictaphone with him. The guardian, apparently, thought it would be useful for Parker's work, and, therefore, he was willing to spend money on that. This cabinet for it was manufactured at the casket factory, my father claimed. You see, it has the name stamped on the back. *American Casket.* It's still in existence, I believe."

"Wait—what?" Leila's mind churned and bubbled, like a wave revealing detritus from the bottom of the sea:

American Casket, Edwina, Lahore, brother. . . . "What was Edwina's last name? What was her brother's name?"

Mamoo looked surprised. "Parker Pickle was his name. Hers would have been the same."

Leila's knees turned to jelly, and she tried to sink onto the sofa behind her, but she missed the cushion by a fraction of an inch and half sat on the armrest. "Ow."

"You seem to have trouble with chairs," Mamoo observed.

"Are you okay?" Samir asked.

Leila slid off the armrest and onto the sofa cushion. "I'm fine, I just—" She looked over at the Dictaphone, and a new thought floated to the surface. "What kind of moth is that?"

"It's a Celestial Moth. He likes the music," Mamoo said. "And the varnish. There's something in it that the moths seem to like; I've often wondered what it might be."

Leila couldn't speak; her mind hummed with the moth and the music.

"You should test it," Samir suggested. "Make your students analyze it as a project."

Mamoo stroked his mustache. "Yes, I might," he said

thoughtfully. "It is odd—very often, at sundown, one or two will flutter through the window and sit on the cabinet. When I play the music, I often get more. You know, those moths never lived in the Punjab until the turn of the century. My father used to claim that Edwina brought them with her."

"That's weird," Leila whispered. It's weird. *It's too weird.* She remembered Edwina playing the music and the moth coming to rest on her violin. It's real magic, Ralph had said. Real. Magic.

"You look like you might vomit," Samir observed.

Leila nodded. "I might," she admitted.

Mamoo reached for a delicate little wastepaper basket decorated with a rose and placed it in front of Leila.

There was no way that she could barf into something so pretty. It sobered her up. "I'm okay," she said, but she was still trying to make sense of it all. "How did you end up with this Dictaphone?"

"My father worked with Parker Pickle, as I mentioned. Mr. Pickle had no children, and when he passed away, he left everything to my father."

"He *died*?" Leila wailed.

"Well, after living in Lahore for forty years," Mamoo replied. He looked over at Samir, who shrugged, as if to say, "I have no idea why she's so emotional."

"Well, what about Edwina?" she asked.

"I assume she died, too, eventually," Mamoo admitted.

The goat let out a miserable-sounding bleat, snapping Leila out of her thoughts about Edwina and Parker and the book and the moth.

"Why don't you leave that goat here with me?" Mamoo suggested. "You can simply tell the family that it ran away. That's true enough."

"Oh—and you won't eat it?"

"My dear girl, I'm not a monster."

"That's fine. Abu will just get another goat," Samir pointed out.

"Oh." Leila winced.

"But you won't be responsible for that one," Samir said, reading her expression.

"Well . . . I will. Kinda." She flopped onto the couch and put her hands in her hair. "I feel like the Angel of Death. I'm, like, the opposite of Kim, aren't I?" she said to Mamoo. "That kid in the novel you gave me."

Mamoo cocked his head. "How so?"

"He fits in everywhere," Leila said. "He can seem Hindu, Muslim, white, Indian, anything. Whereas I never . . . I never know what's going on. I fit in exactly nowhere."

The violin music pulsed through the room while everyone stared at one another in silence.

"My dear, you are American," Mamoo said.

"But that's not anything," Leila countered. "My aunt seems to think it's worse than nothing." She looked over at Samir, half hoping he would contradict her.

He didn't.

"I think that Kim would say that there are some problems that do not have a good solution." Mamoo placed a gentle hand on Leila's shoulder.

"It doesn't make sense," she said. Her voice was quiet and dry, as if it had been ground to fine sand under the weight of her confusion. "It's not fair."

"No," Mamoo agreed. "It's not." His eyes fell on the Dictaphone, where the moth still sat, wings spread, as if it wanted to feel the vibrations of the music.

Edwina's music.

The same notes that Kai had played half a world away.

THE EXQUISITE CORPSE

The notes traveled from one side of the world to the other, and Ralph saved every one of them. Sometimes, he reread all of Edwina's letters in one sitting. Sometimes, he read only his favorite parts. He kept them all in his sweater drawer, in a cigar box wrapped in an intricate pattern of string, so that he would know if anyone disturbed it.

He tried to keep his letters to Edwina cheerful, and her responses were equally happy.

My dear Mole,

Lahore is simply bursting at the seams. Everywhere you turn, the British and locals are building. The streets are thronged with activity such that you can hardly pass. . . .

My dear Mole,

The kindest people live here! I have met a dear girl named Alice Kipling who was born in Bombay. Trix—for she insists that I call her by her pet name—has lived most of her life in India, though she is British. Her brother has promised to take us *on a tour of their father's Wonder House. . . .*

My dear Mole,

Parker and I are planning a concert in our home in a fortnight, and the arrangements for food and drink are straining my nerves. I've had hardly any time to practice my violin. . . .

My dear Mole,

The school is lovely, and the children are absolute dears. Many of them are children of British army officers, and I fear they are lonely little lads. I try to make them smile with tales of the adventures of Girl and Mole.

Yesterday, as he had promised, Ruddy took Parker and me to see the Wonder House. He is a journalist and a bit of a serious fellow, a bit choleric looking, but he has a great wit. His sister tells me that he makes up gruesome stories, and writes quite a bit of poetry. I can't imagine he is much of a poetic soul, but you never can tell, I suppose. On the other hand, his father, Lockwood, is an artist

*through and through! He has a long, regal white
beard and treasures every statue and artifact in the
museum as if it were a gift from the gods themselves. I liked him very much.*

*There is a mighty cannon that stands in front
of the museum, and the children like to sit atop
it and ride it as if it were a dragon. As we were
walking out, I suggested to Ruddy that he write
a poem or story about the children. "For it strikes
me that all young boys are the same," I said. "The
young Irish and Englishmen in my classroom
would be as likely to sit atop a dragon-cannon as
the Hindu and Muslim children there now."*

*Ruddy quite agreed that all young boys are
essentially the same in their love of adventure,
but did not seem terribly interested. I do not
expect that he will ever write anything on the
subject. . . .*

My dear Mole,

*The Britishers are leaving Lahore in droves.
Everyone lives in fear of the hot weather, and*

almost all are departing for Simla. Ruddy is quite insistent with Parker that we must get away. Trix and her mother have already left.

I treasure each and every one of your letters, but I'll own that I grow more homesick by the day. Perhaps a change of scene will do me some good. . . .

My dear Mole,

Ghastly news. My guardian is considering the purchase of a mine and has made plans to journey to India in the coming months. Parker is beside himself with rage. In truth, I feel quite ill at the thought of seeing Melchisedec Jonas again. Now I wish more than ever that I hadn't left the United States. If only I could come back while he is here!

You know that I am heir to a large fortune, but I would truly trade that in a heartbeat for the chance to be free of Melchisedec Jonas. Parker and I speak of little else. He feels the same way I do, but is quite happy in India. I, on the other hand, feel the circles here are very small. Perhaps that is *because I am a woman, and opportunites here are very few. . . .*

After a few months, the letters ceased to arrive. Ralph worried, but he hoped desperately that Edwina was simply busy seeing to her guardian's needs.

Or perhaps she had gone to Simla, where the mail was not as regular.

Or . . .

He tried not to think about other possibilities.

CHAPTER FOURTEEN

Kai

IT WAS AN UGLY thing, with a fat, furry body and two strange palm-frond antennae.

"It's a katydid," Kai said.

"No; it's the moth." Doodle and Kai were bent close, watching the insect through the side of the glass jar. They had placed the jar at the edge of Kai's window.

"Where are its fabulous wings? He's been that way for hours."

"They're still wet," Doodle explained. "It takes time for them to unfurl, for the hemolyph to get to their extremities."

"Hemo-what?"

Doodle translated, "Moth blood. It's not blood, though. It's yellow."

"He's not moving."

"Kai, he's been locked up in a cocoon for who knows how long," Doodle pointed out. "He's tired. Give the bug a break."

Kai laughed.

"What's so funny?"

"Nothing—just—" She shrugged. "'Give the bug a break' sounds like something I would say."

A smile flickered over Doodle's lips as she watched the moth. "Maybe you're rubbing off on me. Go get your violin. Our Celestial wants some music."

Kai scoffed, but she went to the closet and fetched her violin. She tuned it quickly and rosined the bow, then she began to play.

At first, nothing happened, but Kai played on, letting the music fill the room. After a few moments, the moth began to quiver, its antennae moving slowly, as if probing the air around it. The brilliant blue wings opened and slowly beat the still air in the jar.

"Look," Doodle whispered as one wing flickered slightly. Beyond the window, a hush fell over the night as everything paused to listen.

"I've told Mr. Jenkins about your music," Doodle said as Kai played on. "He wants you to play at the fair."

Kai's bow slipped over the strings, letting out a sour screech.

"So you'll do it?"

Kai didn't reply, but she kept on playing, considering. She wasn't sure that she was ready to play in public again. On the other hand, she was sorely tempted to make Pettyfer look like a violin fool *and* a bug fool. She hoped he would crawl into a hole and disappear out of humiliation. Or maybe just burst into flames. But she wasn't at her best, musically, after taking off so much time.

Did it matter? She couldn't decide.

Slowly, slowly, the moth pulsed its wings under the notes from the violin. Doodle snapped a stream of photos with her iPad. And then she unscrewed the top of the jar.

The sudden silence was almost shocking as Kai lifted her bow from the strings. "What are you doing?" she asked, tucking the bow under one arm.

"Setting it free." The moth didn't move, though; perhaps it didn't yet realize what its wings were for. It simply sat on the branch in the jar as if it was perfectly happy there.

"Wait—what? I thought we were taking it to the Lepidoptery Fair!" Spreading her fingers, Kai closed her hand over the top of the jar.

Doodle shook her head. "Now that she has wings, she can't just sit in the jar for two days."

"But—we can't just let Pettyfer win!"

"We have the pictures," Doodle said.

"The real moth is better! And . . and what about the five hundred dollars?"

Doodle stared as if Kai had just started speaking jibberish. "What about the *moth*?"

Kai could feel her face turning red. "Is this because your dad works for the casket company?" Kai demanded. "Are you worried that he'll get fired if we beat Pettyfer? You can't let him scare you!"

"I don't think it's right to keep a moth bottled up, Kai."

They stared at each other for a moment, and this was when Kai realized that Doodle was actually serious. She really *didn't* care about the money. She didn't care about Pettyfer. She didn't care about winning. She cared about the moth. *A stupid moth*. It really was quite stupid; it was still sitting on its leaf in the jar, not even trying to fly away.

Kai's hand tightened on the jar. "It's not wrong to want to win, Doodle," she said. "It's only fair. Pettyfer doesn't *deserve* it."

"I know," Doodle agreed. "So, if he doesn't deserve to, he won't."

The moth fluttered. Even Kai could tell that it was thinking about flying.

Kai felt her skin burn like pavement in the sun, the angry heat she had built up rising, turning to steam, swirling around her. "What about *me*?" she demanded.

Doodle blinked at her. "What *about* you?"

"Huh?"

"Why do you care so much?"

"Because it's—" Kai shook her head. "Because—" She tried to remember why she cared about winning the Lepidoptery Fair. Well, she wanted to beat Pettyfer. She wanted to show him that she was better than he was! She wanted him to see that he was horrible, she wanted him to feel—

To feel—

To feel how I feel, Kai realized, the idea blowing

through her like a breeze. *To know what it's like to be not quite good enough.*

The cloud around her finally lifted, disappearing. And just like that, the contest became just a contest again.

It wasn't proof that she was better than Pettyfer. It didn't mean anything.

Doodle was still watching Kai's face, waiting. Kai thought about Ralph, and how he believed in magic. . . . *There is magic in the world,* Kai thought, and she remembered Doodle's words: *Moths are magical.* There was no doubt about it—*this* moth was very magical.

And magic doesn't do any good if you keep it all bottled up.

Kai lifted her fingers from the jar. "You're right," she said.

The sentence fell to the floor like a boulder, and the moth, who felt the vibration but did not understand its meaning, fluttered through the window and into the night.

There was no doubt about it—this was a big-time small-town event. The friendly old library stood quietly behind a grouping of three large white tents, which shaded several clusters of tables arranged according to subject. People were already milling about, looking at the displays. Kai and Doodle had placed photos of the Celestial Moth—along with illustrations from the diary—on a trifold poster. It stood proudly among the other moth dioramas and reports. In one corner, a long line of children squirmed, watching as a man in a tall striped hat twisted long, colorful balloons into butterflies. At one end of the lawn, the high school a capella group performed a Taylor Swift song. Next to them, a booth was handing out butterfly-shaped cookies and lemonade.

Someone had made a giant—larger than human-size—monarch butterfly puppet, and two people in black bodystockings sweated and tried hard to appear invisible as they made the butterfly dance near the front sidewalk. Lavinia had set up a table selling Luna Juice to benefit the library. There were even games for small children: they could throw beanbags into large wooden chrysalides or have their picture taken with their face appearing in the cut-out hole at the head of a large wooden butterfly. Sidewalk chalk and photos of butterflies and moths were available for anyone who wanted to make street art.

A banner stretched across the tops of the tents: *134th Annual Lepidoptery Fair!*

"This is completely insane." Kai gaped at the people with the giant butterfly puppet as she took a bite of the cookie. "Wow, that's good."

"Yes, insane but good is pretty much what they're going for," Doodle said. "The marching band puts on an amazing show later in the afternoon."

Kai accidentally inhaled a cookie crumb and had to take a swig of lemonade to wash it down. She and Doodle were sitting beneath a tree near the a capella group. "What marching band? There's no marching band," Kai said.

Doodle lifted her eyebrows and pursed her lips, a look that said, *Just you wait.*

"Doodle!" Holding a stack of cookies in one hand and waving with the other, Carlos, the hipster librarian, loped over to join them. He wore a T-shirt bearing an image of a pineapple and tan corduroy jeans, even though the temperature hovered near one hundred degrees. He held up a glass of Luna Juice. "Have you guys tried this stuff?"

"That's my great-aunt who's selling it," Kai told him.

"It's *awesome*. Hey—where's your display?"

"In the tent on the far left," Doodle said as Kai pointed lazily in the general direction of their poster.

"Cool; can't wait to see it. Hey, Professor Hill!" Now Carlos was waving to someone behind them. When Kai turned, she saw a white-haired man in a wheelchair rolling up the front walk. He smiled, and Kai realized that she had seen this man before—when Pettyfer's dad was honking at him from behind the wheel of a Lincoln Navigator. "Professor, I'd like you to meet Miriam Martell and Kai—" Carlos shook his head. "I'm sorry; I realized I don't know your last name."

"It's Grove."

"Kai Grove," Carlos repeated. "And this is Professor Hill. He teaches chemistry at Harlingen College."

"Pleased to meet you." Kai and Doodle stood up to shake his hand, which felt both solemn and a little silly, especially when Doodle explained her nickname. "Are you girls scientists?"

"Yes," Doodle said, just as Kai said, "No."

"Ah! Healthy dissent." Professor Hill nodded and

his eyes crinkled merrily. "We'll see what the evidence shows."

"They did a cool project on Celestial Moths," Carlos told him.

"*Did you?*" The professor's shaggy eyebrows lifted in surprise. Indeed, he was *very* surprised. "How strange. A colleague of mine overseas just wrote to me, mentioning that very moth."

"What did he say?" Doodle asked.

"He had questions about the moth and a local company," Professor Hill said. His tone was oddly serious, and told Kai and Doodle not to ask more. "Well, pardon me—I'd like to have a look at the displays."

"Nice meeting you," Kai murmured as he wove his way into the crowd. He was quite graceful with his wheelchair, maneuvering around obstacles and people who seemed mindless of his existence.

"I want to go look at the other displays, too," Doodle said, and Kai agreed, "Sure."

"I'm gonna go grab more cookies," Carlos told them.

"You've already got five," Doodle pointed out.

"They freeze well." Carlos winked, shoved his glasses

up on his nose, and headed back to the cookie booth as the girls walked toward the tents.

Kai thought that many of the adult projects seemed borderline professional . . . but boring. The kid ones were more colorful, and tended to have lots of pictures. Most people seemed to favor the butterflies. Though there was a really beautiful display with caterpillars and a live monarch just beginning to hatch from a chrysalis. One person did a very detailed explanation of the life cycle of the postman butterfly, another of the gypsy moth. Doodle nodded and exclaimed over each one, even the ones done by kindergartners. She smiled proudly as they passed their own display.

"You should grab your violin," Doodle said. "You'll be performing soon."

"I will?" Kai asked. "I don't remember actually saying I would do it."

"You will," Doodle told her. "That's why your violin case is under the table."

Kai smiled. "I'm doing it for the moths." She grabbed the case.

And then they came to the last table, home of the

display that both had been silently seeking and dreading the entire time.

Well, that sucks, Kai thought as she looked at Pettyfer's display. It wasn't much—just a big shoebox with some sticks in it. *This is what he thinks is going to win?* He'd put it out on a big table, along with several wood-framed mounted moths and butterflies. Looking at them made Kai sick. They were beautiful and amazing—and dead. A wooden sign beside them said, *Frames Courtesy of American Casket.* It was shiny with the famous American Casket odorless, eternal varnish.

"Aren't they nice?" Pettyfer asked, coming up behind her. "Dad had the frames made at the factory."

"They're revolting."

Pettyfer grinned. "That's a nice violin case you've got there," he said. "Did you find it at Goodwill?"

Hilarious, Kai thought. *Just wait until I play, little rich boy. Money can't buy talent.* "Whatever, Pettyfer. It's not like you're going to win with a few framed moths and that lame display."

"That isn't the display," Pettyfer said. "That's just holding the moth. The display is when I show everyone how to preserve and mount it."

"You're going to *kill a moth* at the Lepidoptery fair?" Doodle's jaw hung open.

"You're psycho!" Kai cried, just as something fluttered in Pettyfer's display. The moth had been hidden beneath a leaf, which shifted with its movement.

Doodle gasped.

"Oh, no," Kai whispered.

It was the Celestial Moth.

"You can't kill *that* moth!" Doodle cried. "They're extirpated in this area!"

"Clearly, they aren't," Pettyfer said smoothly. "Just extremely rare. And I'll show everyone how to pre—"

Kai didn't wait for the rest of the sentence—she lunged at the cardboard box. Pettyfer grabbed her sweater, but Doodle tackled him, shouting, "Save him, Kai!" Pettyfer still had a grip on her shirt, which was choking her. She whacked him with her violin case, and he staggered backward just long enough for her to grip the edge of the plastic wrap. The box fell to the floor, and a corner of the plastic came free.

"Get it!" Pettyfer screeched as the moth zigzagged

out. It paused to land on the American Casket sign, where it sat happily for a moment, until Pettyfer lunged at it. Then it fluttered toward the red flowers that grew in front of the library, paused a moment, and flew away.

There was an electric hum beside Kai, and when she looked over, she saw Professor Hill. He was staring after the moth, which had disappeared around the side of the library.

"I'll sue you!" Pettyfer shouted, jabbing a finger at Doodle.

"Go ahead!" Doodle shrieked. "Do it!"

Kai had never seen Doodle so furious, and was so impressed by it that it didn't occur to her to get in between Doodle and Pettyfer. Luckily, it did occur to Carlos, who hurried over to break up the fight.

Kai looked around for Great-Aunt Lavinia. She stood half out of her booth. She had started to come over, and then decided that she wasn't needed. Instead, she had watched the whole scene with an amused smile. She held up a glass of Luna Juice, a toast. Kai smiled a little and turned back to her friends.

Professor Hill looked up at Kai. "Was that . . . a

Celestial Moth?" he asked, breathless.

"Yes," Kai replied.

She expected Professor Hill to say, *Oh, wow! I didn't know there were any still around here!* Instead, he reached out and touched the shiny sign where the moth had landed for a moment. He looked back at Kai. "Take the sign," he commanded, "and follow me."

Kai didn't ask questions; she grabbed the sign and trotted after Professor Hill, who was rolling away at top speed. The hubbub had gone quiet around them, so quiet that Kai could hear the squeak of the balloons as two were twisted together to form a butterfly.

"Hey! Give that back!" Pettyfer shouted. "Get back here! I'll sue you, too! I'll sue all of you!" Carlos was holding him by the shoulders, so it was impossible for him to give chase.

Not that it would have mattered. Kai had the sign in one hand and her violin in the other, and there was no way that she was giving up either one. Her magic book had taught her one thing: she didn't always need to understand what was happening in order to keep moving forward.

She thought about the latest moment in *The Exquisite Corpse*—the part in which Edwina's letters stopped. Do you know what Kai did when she read that?

She wrote: *Unacceptable. I want a happy ending.*

Then she put the book back on the shelf.

Like I said: keep on moving.

THE EXQUISITE CORPSE

I want a happy ending, *Parker thought as he stared at his sister in her coffin. She was wearing her best blue dress. I can't believe this is happening.*

There were very few mourners at the service. Most of the friends they had made were gone to Simla, including Trix and Ruddy, and Melchisedec had not yet arrived in Lahore. Still, several business associates attended the ceremony, including one man who had been introduced as Melchisedec's attorney, but whose blind eye and scarred face suggested another occupation.

The Cathedral Church of the Resurrection was a beautiful pink sandstone structure, newly consecrated. It was not the largest cathedral Parker had ever seen, but it was large enough to whisper the melancholy echo of footeps as the few mourners began to shuffle out.

Melchisedec's "lawyer" moved up the aisle, as if to approach the casket.

"Excuse me," Parker told the man. "I would like a moment alone with my sister before the coffin is sealed."

The man glanced at the casket, where Edwina lay, perfectly still. "I think it is a very elegant casket."

"My guardian very generously provided it."

With a nod, the man donned his hat and turned to leave. His footsteps rang up to the vaulted ceiling.

Parker kneeled at the casket. When the reverend came to speak to Parker, he asked him, too, for a moment alone with his sister.

"Of course," Reverend Allcott said. "Take your time."

"Please accept this donation for the church." Parker passed the reverend a thick roll of bills, and the holy man nodded.

"Thank you," Reverend Allcott replied. "We hope we will one day collect enough to order bells for our tower from England. This will help us."

Once he had left, Parker kneeled by the coffin and prayed silently. Several minutes ticked by. Finally, he whispered, "It's all right."

"Are you sure he's gone?" Edwina asked. She did not open her eyes. She did not stir, except for her lips.

"They all are."

Edwina sat up in the casket, and Parker helped her step down. "I felt that man staring at me. I held my breath."

Parker closed the casket's top.

"This will be buried tomorrow," he told her. "Are you certain you want to do this?"

"Melchisedec is coming." She shook her head. "Do you really think he will wait for me to turn twenty-one, and then allow me to return? You should disappear, too."

"I'm happy here," Parker said. "Besides, you know our 'uncle' has nothing to fear from me. He's bribed every judge in the county; they would never overturn the will. And I don't plan to attempt it."

Edwina smiled sadly at him until he grasped her hand, and they exchanged a warm embrace.

"Here is the ticket for your passage," Parker said, "and enough money to live on for a while. I'll wire you more once you're back in the States. Samir has also provided papers. . . ." Her brother waggled his eyebrows.

"Are you certain that no one will suspect it's me?" Edwina asked.

"You are now Edie Allen," Parker told her. "Samir has also given money to several . . . interested parties." Parker handed Edwina a black canvas bag.

"He's bribed them, you mean," Edwina corrected.

"Really, Edwina. There's no need to be so unsavory." Parker had a deep practical streak, and he knew that when one was fighting fire, it was often best to use fire. "Your trunk has been packed and sent ahead. A proper trunk; not a casket. Samir really is quite a good man." Behind him, light streamed in through the stained-glass window, which glowed luminous blue. Edwina thought of her moths.

She would miss her brother, but this was the only way to truly escape from Melchisedec. It was a magic trick. She would return to Ralph, her dear old mole. He would help her.

Edwina kissed her brother's cheek, and hurried toward the side entrance, where Samir stood waiting for her. He was a native man, very handsome in a bowler hat and smart silver mustache, and he gave a slight bow as she approached.

Edwina clutched her bag in one hand, her violin case in the other. "I'm ready," she said.

CHAPTER FIFTEEN

Leila

MAMOO ANSWERED THE DOOR himself, which surprised Leila so much that she let out a little yelp. Silver eyebrows lifted, Mamoo glanced at Samir. "Are you here for tea?"

"We want a sweet dish!" Wali cried.

Samir hushed his little brother. "Leila wanted to talk to you," he said, just as Leila said, "I've got to tell you something!"

"And so you brought the whole family?" Mamoo crossed his arms and chuckled. He was beginning to appreciate that Leila's intelligence was not the traditional kind; it was more the romantic, creative kind.

"Samir knew the way, Chirragh is our chaperone, and Wali—I have no idea why he's here," Leila explained. Once the seven-year-old caught a whiff of the excitement, he had insisted on coming along. Although it had been explained to him that nothing of interest was happening, he knew a lie when he heard one.

Chirragh went around the house as the children shook off their shoes and hurried toward the long sitting room. Mamoo settled into his chair, Wali bounced on the couch, Samir perched on the end of an ottoman, and Leila stood. The blinds were drawn, but light reached in around the cracks. Mamoo did not turn on a lamp, but there was enough to see by. "Tell me," he said.

"*She didn't die,*" Leila announced. She gestured hugely, as if the whole sitting room were an audience.

"Who didn't die?" Wali asked.

"Edwina Pickle. Everyone thought she died, but she didn't—well, not while she was in Pakistan. India. Whatever."

"Who's that?" Wali asked. Everyone ignored him. Mamoo sat back in his chair and laced his fingers together.

"Why didn't she die?" Wali asked. "Why did people think she did?"

"She and her brother pretended that she had died, so that she could get away from her terrible guardian!"

Leila's words ran together, as if they were in a rush to get out.

Samir's eyebrow stood at attention. "Are we talking about the woman who was playing the violin?" he asked, pointing to the Dictaphone in the corner.

"Yes! They faked her death!" Leila clapped her hands.

"I know that," Mamoo said.

"What?" Leila screeched.

"He said, 'I know that,'" Wali explained.

"That was already in English, Wali, thanks. How could you know?"

Mamoo stood up and crossed the room to the Dictaphone. He pulled open a drawer in the cabinet. "I have her letters." He pulled out a stack of correspondence tied with a faded blue ribbon. "Her brother saved them all, along with his Dictaphone replies, which, I presume, were then typed by my grandfather. I don't know if my father ever realized that they were in the cabinet, but I found them several years ago. I have been asking your father, Samir, to use some of his contacts at the Lahore Museum to see if they would be interested in having them, but he keeps putting it off." Mamoo shook his head. "I don't know why he puts it off."

"You've read the letters?" Leila cried. "What happened to her? Did she marry Ralph?"

"I really have no idea what we're talking about," Samir said.

"I'll explain later," Leila promised, but Mamoo did not want to be rushed.

"My grandfather's employer, Parker Pickle, and his sister, Edwina, were heirs to a very large fortune. Edwina was afraid for her life, and so her brother told everyone that she died of typhoid and had her casket buried in the cemetery. But she returned to the United States, and her brother paid for her to go to college. Eventually, she got married—"

"To Ralph?" Leila cried.

Mamoo looked at her curiously. "To a man named Ralph Flabbergast."

"I knew it! I knew it!" Leila danced around the room, and Wali took the opportunity to join her, also shouting, "I knew it!" although he had not known it, not remotely.

"At any rate, it's very interesting. It seems that, upon his sister's 'death,' Parker Pickle *should* have become the heir to a large fortune—but he never collected it, as he was not formally named in the will. Not that he seems to have tried very hard. So his guardian—"

"Melchisedec!" Leila cried.

"You should say Alhamdulillah," Wali instructed her, assuming she had sneezed.

Mamoo narrowed his eyes. "Yes, Melchisedec Jonas— he retained control of the company. Parker very clearly hoped that Edwina's daughter would someday inherit the fortune, but I doubt she ever did."

"Oh, they had a baby!" Leila wished she had brought *The Exquisite Corpse* with her; she would have given it a kiss.

"Well, the whole thing has recently come to my attention because I had the shellac on the cabinet tested, as you suggested, Samir. It contains a derivative of Scarlet Catsbane, which is what the moths so enjoy. It is their primary food. But it can cause respiratory and skin problems for some humans, especially those with lung weaknesses. The American Casket website says that they still use their one-hundred-year-old preservation formula, so I wrote to them, warning them that their shellac might be dangerous, and I received a rather nasty reply."

"But—Melchisedec Jonas can't still be alive?" Leila asked.

"The letter," Mamoo said, pursing his lips, "was from someone calling himself Pettyfer Jonas Sr."

Leila was shocked. "What a jerk!"

"Indeed," Mamoo agreed.

The room fell silent.

"Can we have a sweet now?" Wali asked.

Leila looked up at him. She had forgotten he was there. She had forgotten about Samir, too, who was looking at her with an expression of patient bewilderment, as if he wasn't sure what was happening, but understood it was important and had faith that he would hear an explanation later.

In the kitchen, something clinked.

"Do you smell that?" Mamoo asked as a fragrant scent wafted past. "Ah! My cook is quite good. Of course, he can't compare with Chirragh."

Chirragh makes the best goat in Lahore, Shireen had said. Leila shuddered when she remembered that Chirragh was supposed to buy a new goat today. There was no way to stop him . . .

"It smells like *gajar halwa*!" Wali cried as a servant opened a door and entered the room pushing a tea cart.

"Oh, good," Samir said.

But Leila's thoughts whirled. "Wait," Leila said, holding up a hand. "Wait."

"Wait for what?" Samir asked, but Mamoo hushed him.

Thoughts were colliding like atoms in Leila's mind; she was burning with the friction of them. *Chirragh is trustworthy—he has been with the family his whole life. Edwina in the coffin. Chirragh's lamb is delicious. Edwina escaped. The goat is under a death sentence.*

She looked up at them. Her face was completely changed—it was shining with the light from all those thoughts. "I have an idea," she announced.

Three days later, Leila was in the Awans' backyard, standing in the shade of the mango tree. Samir, Wali, and Babar Taya stood beside her, and the goat paced, finally letting out a raw bleat. It was her goat, Flower. Chirragh had brought her back.

Chirragh squatted, sharpening a knife on a stone.

Every now and again, he would pause to test the blade against his thumb. To Leila, the blade looked fine as a razor.

"I do not enjoy this," Babar Taya admitted. "Some people simply lay their hands on the knife, and then allow the servant to butcher the animal. But I don't feel that I should ask Chirragh to do something that I am unwilling to do myself." He sighed and looked at Leila. "I do hope that this won't be too upsetting for you."

"It's part of my culture," Leila said nervously. Her heart throbbed, as if it were tender with a bruise, and the heat made her head buzz. She did not want to stay, either. She would rather be inside with her aunt and Rabeea, but she felt much as Babar Taya did. This mess was her fault. She couldn't just run away now, no matter what.

She took a deep breath, inhaling the scent of rotting mango. The rains had come last night, pouring down thick as snowflakes, hard as gravel. This morning, the ground was wet, and all of the leaves were washed clean.

Finally, Chirragh held up the knife and nodded curtly. He held the blade, offering the handle to Babar Taya. Her uncle's fingers reached—

"What! What's all this?" Mamoo barreled into the yard, closely followed by Asif and another servant, who were weighted down with a large box. "Nephew, I have come to tell you that this is your final chance to review these documents for the Lahore Museum. Otherwise, I will ship them to America today!"

Babar Taya's eyes were wide at the sight of the box. "It's Eid," he said.

"My friend is traveling to the States, and has agreed to take them. There is a museum that is interested!"

Babar Taya looked distressed. "I had no idea there were so many documents!"

"I have three more boxes," Mamoo announced. "But it is just as simple to send them to America, where they may be of greater value."

"Leave them here, Mamoo," Babar Taya said. "I'll look through them and send them along this week."

"My friend leaves tonight!" Mamoo pointed to the box. "Either you take them to the museum now, or I will ship them to America today!"

"Mamoo, don't be unreasonable. . . ."

"*I* am unreasonable? This is absurd! I have been asking

about this for three years! I want this taken care of—right now."

Babar Taya seemed to think it over. Finally, he gave a little flick of the hand. "I think that would be best," he said. "Yes, send them to America."

Leila gulped.

Chirragh held out the blade again.

"Eh? What's this?" Mamoo asked. "Am I not the elder? Should not the honor of the sacrifice go to me?"

Babar Taya looked surprised. "You've never wanted to do it before, Mamoo."

"Nonsense!" He gestured toward Chirragh, who held the knife toward Mamoo.

"Abu?" A screen door slammed, and Samir burst out into the yard. "Abu! I'm sorry, but there's a man on the telephone who insists on speaking with you right away. He says he is calling from Hong Kong. He said it was quite urgent—something about servers being hacked—"

The color drained from Babar Taya's face, and Leila felt a stab of worry. But Babar Taya turned to Mamoo. "You don't mind doing the honor?" he asked, glancing toward the goat.

"I insist," Mamoo said, in a voice that left no room for doubt.

Babar Taya murmured a quiet prayer, thanked Mamoo—who waved him away—and then darted into the house. Chirragh gave Mamoo the knife, and Mamoo motioned to the servants to place the box on the ground.

Leila untied the goat. "Good-bye," she said, throwing her arms around the goat's neck. "Don't be afraid."

The goat let out a terrified scream as Asif picked her up. Mamoo opened the lid of the box, and Asif placed her inside. Mamoo barked directions to Asif, and he and Mamoo's driver lifted the box. Asif smiled at Leila, his dark mustache trembling as if he was laughing very quietly as he carried the box to Mamoo's car.

Chirragh jutted his chin, and Mamoo's whiskers twitched. "I'll be back in time for dinner," he said, and then turned to follow the box.

Leila smiled after him. "I like that crazy old guy."

Samir nodded. "He's a good man."

Wali looked up at Leila. "But what are we going to eat?"

"It's called seitan," Leila said. "I had Asif pick some up

at the international store. It's made of wheat, but it tastes like meat. Once Chirragh is done with it, you won't know the difference."

"And what about Allah? Won't he be angry?" Wali's black eyes were huge.

"Mamoo has given money to the poor for our family," Samir explained. "No one will go hungry because of this goat." He grinned at Leila. "Furthermore, it was a sadaqa," he said.

"Sadaqa?" Leila repeated. A blessing. A good thing. *Well . . . it sort of is. Like feeding the pigeons.*

"It was an adventure!" Wali cried, which made Leila giggle, although she guessed it was true. It was small, and it was kind of . . . *weird.* And there were parts of it that she didn't understand.

It wasn't at all like a Dear Sisters adventure, but it was real, and it was magical, and it was hers. She wished she could tell someone about it—Ta'Mara, or Aimee, or even Nadia. But none of them would ever believe it. None of them had the right kind of imagination.

But she did.

Leila looked up at the sky. The clouds were small and

choppy, but the sky was clear. The smoke had lifted; the rain had washed it all away.

THE EXQUISITE CORPSE

FALLS RIVER SENTINEL

Mark and Ellen Grove (nee Flabbergast) are delighted to announce the birth of their son, Walter Isaac Grove, on July 10, 1968. He weighed seven pounds, ten ounces, and was seventeen inches long.

Walter Grove is the first great-grandchild of Ralph and Edie Flabbergast (nee Allen). The couple would like to invite the public to an ice-cream social to celebrate the birth, as well as the occasion of their fiftieth wedding anniversary. The party will be held on the town green, Saturday, July 28, at 2 p.m. All are welcome.

If you don't believe me, check the county records.

CHAPTER SIXTEEN

Kai

IF YOU DON'T BELIEVE me, check the county records, Kai read.

She stood up.

She sat down.

She stared at the book.

Kai stood up again. Adrenaline coursed through her body; she wanted to move, but there was nowhere to go. She was seated at a table in the center of the small, old library.

"You okay?" Carlos asked from his place behind the service desk. He was looking at her over the tops of his black-framed hipster glasses.

Kai blinked at him. How to explain that a magic book had just told her—what? That her father was related to

Ralph and Edwina? She plopped back down into her chair and looked over at Doodle, who peered at her curiously. "Is there a tack in your chair?"

Kai spun *The Exquisite Corpse* and pushed it at her friend. "Look."

Doodle scanned the names. "I don't get it. What is this?"

"Walter Grove," Kai said, pointing. "Walter Grove. That's my dad."

"Oh my gosh!" Doodle stood up, her eyes bugging, froglike, from her head. Then she looked over at Carlos, who was watching them with narrowed eyes. *What?* He mouthed. Doodle shook her head and sat back down. "Ralph Flabbergast is Walter's great-grandfather. . . ."

Kai was tryng to work out what it meant. She couldn't quite—

"They're *your* great-great-grandparents!" Doodle hissed.

"It's so weird. . . ." Kai shook her head. "It's so weird. . . ." Her thoughts pinged off of one another like marbles in a jar.

Doodle stared at her.

"What?" Kai asked.

Doodle kept staring at her, like she was trying to beam a thought across the table.

"What is it?" Kai asked. "Don't just think it at me—tell me."

"Don't you get it?"

"I thought I got it. . . ." She looked down at the book. *They're your great-great-grandparents,* she told herself, *just like Doodle said.*

"*You're the heir,*" Doodle said.

"I'm the air?" Kai's brain wasn't really working at top speed. It's like when you put too much stuff in a blender, and the blade just spins, but nothing gets pureed. Kai thought Doodle was working on a metaphor, something along the lines of "You're the wind beneath my wings," but she couldn't quite make sense of it.

"The heir *to the fortune,*" Doodle explained. "American Casket. You should own it. *You!*"

Carlos leaned against their table, arms folded. "You girls are freaking me out with all of the whispering," he said. "What are you plotting?"

Doodle took one look at Kai's blank, stunned

expression, and said, "Carlos, we need to do a search of the local birth and death records."

He shrugged. "Sure."

"But . . . we can never prove it," Kai said slowly. "Everyone thinks Edwina died in Lahore."

"You have the book!" Doodle cried.

"A magic book is hardly proof, Doodle."

"This conversation is mighty interesting," Carlos observed calmly.

At that moment, the front door huffed open and Professor Hill wheeled into the library. A large manila envelope sat across his knees. "Carlos! I have a present for you!"

"What is it?"

Professor Hill steered right up to him. "I know that you're interested in preserving historical documents, so I've brought you some correspondence between prominent local residents."

A very strange feeling crept over Kai's scalp. "Who—" she whispered. "Who is it from?"

Professor Hill smiled. "Hello, Kai. Doodle. An old friend and colleague of mine in Pakistan has sent me these letters." Opening the flap, he pulled out a bundle of letters bound with a pale ribbon. "These were written at the turn of the twentieth century, between a woman named Edwina Pickle and her brother, Parker. Heirs to the American Casket fortune. And speaking of that! This same overseas friend has been concerned about the shellac used at the American Casket Company, so I have sent that sign we took to a laboratory. We should have results in a few days." His ran his hands through his white hair, which continued to stand on end. "But I have a feeling that those results might make someone very unhappy." Professor Hill cackled gleefully.

"You sound like you *hope* the results make someone unhappy," Doodle told him.

"I can neither confirm nor deny that." Professor Hill looked at her very seriously, and then chuckled. "Oh, hell—I'll confirm it. I hope Pettyfer Jonas spends a little time in prison for putting people at risk. I wish they could bring his old great-grandfather back to life and throw him behind bars, too."

Doodle wanted to hear all about this, of course, but when she looked over at her friend, she saw that Kai was in a daze. She hadn't heard a word about the shellac. Doodle reached for Kai's hand and held it, but Kai barely felt her fingers. She wasn't attached to her body. She had floated out, somewhere beyond the ceiling, into the bright blue sky, and beyond.

"Lavinia!" Kai shouted as she flung open the front door. "Lavinia!"

Her aunt shone like a shell on the dark green velvet couch. She wore a brilliant turquoise and pink tunic over white jeans, and smiled as Kai, disheveled and sticky with sweat, burst into the living room, demanding, "What was the name of your uncle's wife?"

Lavinia made no comment on Kai's wild-eyed looks or rude question. Instead, she gestured to the armchair across the room. "Kai, sugar, look who's here," she said gently.

A woman in a loose gray dress stood up. She had short dark hair, clipped into a bob that reached just below her ears, and warm gray eyes.

"Mom!" Kai raced to her mother and flung her arms around her, pressing her cheek to the soft folds of her mother's old linen sundress. She smelled of coffee and baby powder. She had her arms around Kai and was kissing the side of her head, murmuring, "Buggy, buggy, my little love bug," which was her pet name for Kai. "I've missed you so much. When did you get so *tall*? What happened? It's only been a few weeks!"

"You can't stop them growing." Lavinia's eyes sparkled.

"What are you *doing* here?" Kai asked. "Why didn't you tell me you were coming?"

"Well, I didn't know I was," Kai's mother said. "But I had a Skype interview with Browning Solutions last week, and it went so well that they flew me in for an in-person interview yesterday."

Lavinia perched at the edge of her sofa cushion. "Where are they located, exactly? What part of Houston?"

"It's right by Rice University," Schuyler replied. "It's about a ninety minute drive out here. I was supposed to fly back tonight, but they offered me the job—"

"They did?" Kai asked. "To work in Houston?"

"Kai, honey." Schuyler's voice was gentle, and she took her daughter's hands. "They need someone to start soon. In a few weeks. This is a great opportunity, and I hope that you will—"

"Fine! Great! Let's move to Houston!"

"—uh . . ." Schuyler stood still for a moment, blinking at her daughter. "Um." She looked uncertainly at Lavinia, who shrugged. Schuyler looked back at Kai. "I had sort of prepared a speech. . . ."

"Oh! Sorry." Kai sat down on the chair and looked expectantly at her mother. Lavinia pushed herself backward on the couch and did the same.

"Well—maybe it isn't necessary. . . . But . . . uh . . . Kai, the schools are very good, and a few people have suggested violin teachers."

Kai put up a hand. "Look, Mom—about that." She pressed her lips together, hesitating as her ears grew hot with shame. "I want to keep playing," she said in a low voice. *I have to,* she thought. *I can't just put away my father's violin forever.* "But I don't want to be as—*intense*—about it anymore."

"That's wonderful, honey. I'm so glad."

It was Kai's turn to be nonplussed. The air conditioner hummed. A truck rolled by outside. "What?" Kai asked.

"Buggy, you love the violin. You always have. But all of that intensity—that wasn't healthy."

"But—what about Dad? What about his dream, and . . . and having opportunities he never had?"

"Kai, your father loved the violin, but his father forbade him to play it. He said that it was taking time from his academics," Schuyler explained.

"He used to practice over here, sometimes," Lavinia put in. "It was his little secret." Her eyes twinkled.

Schuyler took Kai's hand. "Walter wanted you to have the opportunity he never did—the opportunity to be whatever you wanted to be. I like it when you play because you seem to enjoy it. But I think we both got . . . carried away, maybe. It shouldn't be about being the best. It's about the *music*."

Kai then leaned back in her chair and stared at the ceiling.

It's about the music.

It's about the moths.

And she laughed with a sound like bells ringing, clear and loud. She looked at Lavinia, then at her mother.

Everything was happening so fast. *They don't even know about Edwina and Ralph! They don't know about American Casket.* "I have to tell you something," she announced. "You might want to sit down."

"Is everything okay?" Schuyler asked, turning to Lavinia.

"As far as I know it is." Lavinia looked concerned and confused.

"It's all okay," Kai reassured them. "It's great, in fact. It's just—unusual news. Highly unusual. And it's kind of a long story."

"Well, then," Lavinia said, standing up and straightening her tunic. "I'd better get us all some of your world-famous Luna Juice."

CHAPTER SEVENTEEN
Leila

"WHAT ARE YOU LAUGHING AT?" Samir asked as he stood in the doorway to Leila's bedroom.

She was sitting on the red coverlet, her silver laptop in her lap. She turned the screen to show her sister being doused with water by a baby elephant.

Samir walked the twenty-three steps to take a better look. "Is that Nadia?"

"She has a blog," Leila explained. "It's kind of fun to read, actually. I'll send you the link."

"You must miss her a lot."

Leila thought it over. She hadn't missed Nadia at all at the beginning of the trip. In fact, she had missed her friends more. But, over the past three days, Leila had started thinking about her sister. She had wondered if

Aimee really did have more in common with Nadia than with Leila. She had started to see that, even though she had known Aimee a long time, they were really very different. And Leila had started to wonder if, maybe, her real Best Friend was still out there, waiting for her. "I do miss her."

"Well, you're going home in a few days."

"Yeah."

"What's Houston like?" Samir reached for the chair by the desk and sat down in it.

"Gah. Boring."

"Not as boring as here, I'll bet."

"What? It isn't boring here!" Leila closed the computer. "There are parrots in the trees and donkey carts and crazy dressed-up goats and fakirs and *your squirrels have stripes* and—how can you think it's boring? People are always visiting; there's always something happening. It's—it's *magical*."

Samir smiled. "I'll bet Houston would seem magical to me."

Leila thought about her safe little neighborhood, the pretty park nearby with the community swimming pool and skate park, and the lady down the street who planted her whole yard with blooming cornflowers. She thought about the tornado sirens that wailed every night at six, just to make sure they were working, and the times that the sky would turn black with thunderclouds bitten by flashes of lightning. She thought about the strange traditions that her family took part in: the rodeo, the Houston Moonlight Bicycle Ramble, the way they could hop into the car and be at the beach in Galveston in forty-five minutes. *It isn't such a bad place to live,* she decided. It wasn't like Precious City, California, or the Dear Sisters' mansion . . . but it had magic all its own.

"Yeah—you'd like it," Leila said.

Samir smiled. "Do you want to go downstairs? Everyone's watching *Pakistan Idol.*"

Leila stood up. "Did they kick that awful guy off yet? The one with the beard?"

"Don't say that in front of Rabeea—he's her favorite!" Samir scolded as they walked toward the stairs. They could already hear Wali shouting at the television set.

Leila missed her family, but *this* was her family, too. It

had taken time, but she felt at home here. Her trip hadn't been what she had expected, but it had shown her where she belonged.

Everywhere.

Epilogue

WELL, THERE ISN'T MUCH more to the story. Leila returned home and discovered that Nadia was still often annoying, and that, in spite of her epiphany in Pakistan, the whole world had not turned magical overnight. Ta'Mara had a new boyfriend, and she talked about him all of the time. Aimee was obsessed with her new part in the fall ballet, so she didn't hang out with Nadia as much as Leila had feared she would. And Nadia was still . . . Nadia. She had decided to start a nonprofit—something about helping baby ducks—and was busily assembling a robot in her spare time.

Leila never started a blog, but she did keep in touch with Samir, who sent emails with photos of Wali, and Rabeea's art, and even Mamoo and the goat, which had grown quite fat in Mamoo's care.

Babar Taya had said that Leila could take *The Exquisite Corpse* with her to America, and she had, but nothing new appeared. Over time, the words began to fade; a week before school was to begin in the fall, it was completely blank except for the first page. It was just as she had found it. "Nice try," she told the book when she discovered the change. "But I know you're still magic."

Kai's copy of the book also faded, but she also stubbornly clung to the belief that the book was magic. "I have a witness," she informed the book. "Doodle knows all about you, wise guy."

When Professor Hill sent the lab results and the copy of Mamoo's email detailing his concerns about Scarlet Catsbane to the local paper, the small-town press had a field day with the fact that Pettyfer Jonas Sr., knew that the shellac used at American Casket could cause problems for asthmatics, and did nothing. He was quickly ousted as president, and Doodle's father was chosen to take his place. When Scarlet Catsbane was replaced with a harmless compound, his lungs recovered quickly and he found he was rarely ever sick. In addition, the new shellac actually cost less and lasted longer. Unharvested, the field of Scarlet Catsbane grew and bloomed behind the factory, and Doodle spotted *three* Celestial Moths there one evening, a fact that she dutifully reported to the Lepidoptery

Society at their monthly meeting.

Once the judge reviewed the proof of Edwina's life and checked it against the will her parents had made, Kai became the official heir to the American Casket fortune. The money was held in trust for her, but once she turned twenty-one, the money would be hers.

Kai and her mother moved to Houston. They often went to visit Lavinia and Doodle on weekends, and Kai would play her violin in the evenings. They found a sweet little one-story house in a lovely, safe neighborhood with a community pool and a skate park nearby. They were right next door to a woman who had planted her whole yard with cornflowers. School was set to start in a week, and Kai had the strangest feeling that she would make friends there. Maybe even a Best Friend. Doodle had shown her how.

Kai knew now that every story—even her own—held its own magic, and all she had to do was keep turning the pages until the eventual very real, very happy ending.

Acknowledgments

I WOULD LIKE TO gratefully acknowledge the people who made it possible for me to write this book, and those who made it impossible for me to give up.

Thank you to An Na, who gently steered me away from the wrong story; to Mark Karlins, who steered me toward the right one; to Rita Williams-Garcia, who helped me understand the characters; and to Kathi Appelt, who brought me all the way home.

I would like to thank James Patterson for his generosity, which enabled me to dedicate myself to this project. Thank you to the staff of the National Museum of Funerary History, who helpfully provided information on nineteenth-century casket factories.

I must thank my husband, Ali Usman, and my other Lahori advisors and readers: Aimen Khan, Uzma Sajid, and Annum Khan. I would also like to thank other early readers: Kathryn Gaglione, Marguerite Belkin, Ellen Wittlinger, Nancy Werlin, Pat Collins, and Liza Ketchum.

I have a special velvet-lined box of thanks for Rosemary Stimola and Kristen Pettit, who not only believed in this story, but have believed in *me* for a long, long time.

And, of course, thanks and love to the Allies in Wonderland.